P9-BZU-950

Johanna's Journal #1

Melody of My Heart

Carrie Bender

A. B. Publishing
Ithaca, Michigan

Illustrations:

Julie Martin/James Converse

Cover Art:

Julie Martin/James Converse
copyright © 2003
by A. B. Publishing, Inc.

All Rights Reserved

Printed in the United States of America

Published by:
A. B. Publishing, Inc.
Ithaca, MI 48847
www.abpub.com

*W*hile the facts about the Johnstown flood are true, this story is fiction. Any resemblance to persons living or dead is purely coincidental.

Contents

A Note From Dora Bontrager

In this book you won't find any of my own journal jottings. This is the journal of Johanna Montgomery of Johnstown, Pa., starting on January 1, 1888. Johanna was the stepsister of my great, great, great aunt on my Papa's side. Papa was an outsider married to my mother before she joined the Amish church. Johanna's journal was found in the attic of an old stone house on the outskirts of Johnstown, in an ancient horsehair trunk. The house belonged to her great nephew, and was just recently dismantled. The trunk was found way back in a corner behind a built-in "kammerli" (closet). My mother sent me the old journal, knowing I'd be interested in copying it. Husband Matthew was as interested. After doing a bit of research, we discovered that the founder of Johnstown, Amish man Joseph Johns (or Schantz, in Dutch) was a distant relative of his—a great, great, great, great uncle to him (or something like that). That made things even more interesting to us. Johnstown was named after Mr. Johns.

What a tragedy that big flood was, leaving over two thousand dead, and twenty-seven thousand homeless; indeed, it's unfathomable. I hope I'll someday get a chance to see the flood museums they have in Johnstown—maybe the next time we go to Pa.

This journal isn't only about the flood—it's a young girl's hopes, dreams, and romance, too.

Best Wishes,
Dora Bontrager

PART ONE
Johanna's Journal

It's Sunday afternoon on New Year's Day, a good time to start the new journal Aunt Rolla gave me for Christmas. It's cozy here in the library curled up in Papa's old armchair. A cheery fire crackles in the fireplace, sending sparks up the chimney and out into the snowy white world. Pearl, our beloved old house-keeper, just brought in a bowl of popcorn she had popped. She announced that there's a real blizzard in the making. The wind is howling down over the mountain sending the swirling snow into every nook and cranny of our yard and orchard. It is heaping the plowed garden high with drifts and adorning the row of fir trees bordering our lane with mounds of sparkling whiteness.

My eighteen-year-old sister Julie, who is a year younger than I am, is curled up on the wide cush-ioned window seat, reading *Pilgrim's Progress*. She looks up every now and then to gaze out the window through the whirling whiteness to the town of Johnstown below.

I'd love to take a walk downtown after the snow stops. I'd like to walk along the banks of the Little Conemaugh River to see the beauty of the new fallen snow transforming everything, covering the soot and grime that the iron works furnaces put out. But I wouldn't be able to go far before my lame leg would begin to ache. Quite likely Aunt Rolla, who never misses a thing, would see me limping along, and come out on her porch and call out, "Johanna, you get in here this minute!" There would be nothing else to do but obey (for no one ever disobeys Aunt Rolla, in whose tongue is the law of kindness, greatly spiced with tartness). She'd hustle me into a chair in front of the fire with my leg on a hassock. She'd wrap me in a quilt; bring me a cup of hot chocolate. Then she'd send meek Uncle Otto scurrying out to the barn to hitch Old Dobbin to the sleigh to drive me home, all the while scolding me for my foolishness in venturing out into the storm. (Sigh!)

My longing to be free of my burdensome handicap is overwhelming sometimes. But I know it's a cross I'll have to bear all my life, and I intend to carry that cross with a smile. Pearl has been with our family so long she seems like a second mother to Julie and me. She has often told me of what a shock it was to her and my parents to see my little clubfoot when I was born. The three surgeries I had to go through were painful for them as well. I can't remember the surgeries that did not take my handicap away.

I don't wish to complain, for it could have been a lot worse. I still have so much for which to be thankful. For one, I'm thankful for good, kind Christian parents like Papa and Mama, Will and Melda Montgomery. They try in all things to lead Julie and me in the paths of uprightness and are good examples to us in everything they do. They belong to the "old school" if anyone does—I'm sure their adversities have helped mold them into what they are. They have gone through so much: First was the baby daughter who died of pneumonia at six months of age two years before I was born. Then my little five-year-old brother Frederick died of diphtheria eight years ago. The diphtheria epidemic hit so swiftly and unexpectedly that year. We all felt so helpless and terrified when Frederick came down with it. Dozens of children had already died of it. Oh! How we prayed for God to heal him. But God's ways are higher than our ways. The tears still flow as I write of this . . . I'll never forget the sight of him in his little coffin—his mop of golden curls, his angelic little face. Julie and I are dark haired and brown eyed. Frederick was blonde and had big blue eyes. He was the sunshine of our home. We all loved him so! In the twinkling of an eye, or so it seemed to us, the darling and pet of our home was gone. There's a saying—"Earth has no sorrow that Heaven can't heal," but we still sometimes long to see him. Our hearts ache to think that we'll never see him again in this life. The minister at church this morning spoke of the resurrection. I wondered: Would Frederick still be a little five-year-old boy? Somehow, I find myself wishing he would be.

I think I've told you enough for now, dear journal, for a wintry twilight is descending. Pearl has just been in to light the kerosene lamps, telling us that supper will be ready in twenty minutes. The snow is still coming down thick and fast and the wind is howling around the eaves as mightily as ever. How thankful it makes me feel for a warm and cozy home!

I woke up this morning to the sound of someone whistling a merry tune down below. So I "sprang" to the window (if a lame leg really allows one to spring), and saw our good friend and neighbor, Vincent Costlow energetically clearing our front walk. He was shoveling so fast that he made the snow fly. I couldn't resist knocking on the windowpane to attract his attention and wave to him. He paused from shoveling long enough to pack a handful of snow into a ball. He drew back his arm, aiming it at me. I didn't believe for a minute he really would throw it, but I ducked down anyway.

Vincent has been a good friend of our family ever since both of his parents were killed in a train wreck ten years ago. He was thirteen. He came to live with his aunt and uncle who also live on the hillside on the outskirts of Johnstown. Papa has been like a father to him these years. His uncle is an invalid and unable to fill that role.

We all love Vincent, and he loves us. But I think there's something a little more than "brotherly and sisterly" love brewing between Vincent and Julie. We tell each other everything. She confides in me the innermost desires and longings of her heart. So far I've seen no reason to discourage her in her dreaming. I think Vincent feels the same way towards her and is just waiting until she's a little older to speak out. Countless times I've seen a certain tenderness in his eyes when she smiles at him. He's a handsome, honest-hearted young man, and I can't blame Julie one bit for adoring him. In fact, if it weren't for Julie, I think I'd "set my cap" for him myself. But I must stop myself from thinking along these lines because my heart begins to ache, worse than my leg has ever ached. I must take care this heart of mine will not come into a vulnerable position where it can be broken in two. No, I wish only the best for Julie. And I'll never mention this to anyone but you, old journal, and probably never again even to you. I'm sure that Mama and Papa also hope that things will work out for Julie and Vincent to be married. Certainly, they are not in the dark about the way the wind is blowing. Julie will make the perfect wife for him—she is lovely and sweet-faced, and even sweeter in character.

I once heard Aunt Rolla (when she didn't know I could overhear) say to a neighbor that both of us girls have inherited our mother's marvelous beauty and sweetness of disposition. It brought a warm glow to my heart that lasted for days. Now that I am older and wiser, I know that I have a lot of "growing in grace" to do before I can begin to compare to Mama's worthy character.

After breakfast was over, Mama poured a mug of coffee for Vincent, and invited him in, as I am sure he had expected her to. He didn't hesitate for a minute as he stamped the snow off his galoshes outside the doorway. He said he wouldn't need to be invited twice. Pearl brought him a plate of muffins, saying he needed a "little bite of something to 'chirk' him up." Julie and I got out our coats, scarves and gloves, wanting to get some fresh air and see the wondrous beauty of the newly fallen snow.

Vincent said, half jokingly, "Better bundle up warmly if you don't want to freeze your noses and toeses." He was speaking to us both (between mouthfuls of muffins.) But later, when we came back from a tramp around the barn and orchard, and he was finishing the clearing of the driveway, he seemed to have eyes only for Julie. And, indeed, she made a striking picture, with her cheeks rosy from the cold, laughing with bright eyes, and a few curls escaping from under her hood. She said, rather coquettishly, "Will you help us make a snowman?" And Vincent fell to, helping us to roll a ball the size of a bushel basket for the base and several nearly as large for the rest. Julie got one of Papa's old hats. Vincent got a handful of coal from the coal bin for the features. I found a scarf and a broom. We were all merrily shouting with laughter at the rakish appearance of the finished snowman, when Papa came round the corner of the carriage house.

"I'm sorry to interrupt your merry fun," he said, half apologetically. "But I just received a message that there's a poor family down on Main Street in need of help. The mother gave birth to a baby last night. The other children are most all down with the flu. The house is cold because the shabby roof of their coal shed blew off last night. The coal is wet and buried under a great drift of snow. The father injured his back last week . . ."

"Enough said!" I cried out, thinking I couldn't bear to hear more. "What can we do?"

Papa laughed then, and said, "That's my girl! I want you girls to help Pearl cook an ample meal for the family, and Vincent, would you be willing to come with me to see what we can do to get the house warm, and to repair the roof?"

We all scurried off to do as bidden—we peeled potatoes and made biscuits and dried beef gravy, dried corn simmered in milk, and a great big pot of pork and sauerkraut. Julie mixed a batch of molasses cookies, and I made some vanilla pudding. Pearl murmured all the while about the hungry little urchins and the poor little mother. When the meal was ready, Papa and Vincent came round with the horses hitched to the sleigh. Julie and I bundled up and piled on with the kettles and pans of food. We had a fast, exhilarating sleigh ride with the wind in our faces and the trees and buildings whizzing by. The sleigh bells rang merrily. (Vincent was driving; we always have more speed when he drives.) In almost no time at all, we were pulling up in front of the cheap pine-board house and carrying everything inside. The house was warm by then. It sure was a satisfying feeling seeing all those hungry little children gathering around the long pine plank table with their plates and spoons, and relishing everything they ate.

The mother was in bed, of course, and she shed tears of joy at our "wondrous kindness" as she put it. I got to hold her little bundle, a tiny girl named Effie, wrapped in layers and layers of shawls, and a little yarn cap on her head. I think it made us all happy to be able to help them. Truly, it is "more blessed to give than to receive."

Papa and Mama are always thinking of ways to help those less fortunate than us. We girls aid and abet them as much as we can. They are quite a team, and will surely get their reward someday for everything they have done. I said as much to Vincent as I helped him to unhitch the horses. He said, "Doing good to others is a reward unto itself." And I'm sure he's right, even if it were just for the good feeling you have in your heart after doing things for others.

I must bid you "good-night" now, old journal, for it's time to "bank the fires" for the night. It almost seems like a luxury to have a bright and cozy fire of my own in the fireplace in my room. Papa has said more than once already that since the mountains are so close and the logs free for the chopping—(and then he adds, with a twinkle in his eyes) and a strong-armed young man like Vincent jumping for the chance to supply firewood for the girls, it would never do to make them sleep in icy cold rooms. He glances mischievously at Julie as he says it. She blushes a deeper shade of pink every time. Sometimes I feel almost torn in two—on the one hand wanting something so much for your sister, and on the other hand, not wanting it at all, for then she would leave home and I'd lose my best friend. Even though she'd probably not move far, we'd not be half as close to each other anymore because Vincent would come first with her. Oh well, I won't worry about it now. "All things work together for good to them that love the Lord and are called according to His purpose." I'll just enjoy her while I can, and make up with her after each spat and fallout we have, and afterward, love her more dearly than ever. Finally, goodnight!

January 3

These past few weeks I have been spending my Saturdays in the employ of the Reverend D. L. Hollis and his wife. They live in the parsonage near the park just off Main Street. They are a kind, elderly couple—both epitomes of kindness, virtue and saintliness. I spend the morning there doing the weekly Saturday cleaning. Then I help to prepare the noon meal. In the afternoon there is office work to be done, and after that we have tea. That's my favorite part of being there—lingering at the table to talk, for we find ourselves drawn into lengthy conversations and discussions. Dr. and Mrs. Dave (as I call them and most everyone else does, too) welcome any questions I have for them. I find myself looking forward immensely to these stimulating, inspiring and informative talks. There is so much to learn from them. They have a lifetime of experience and wisdom. I would not hesitate to confide in them about anything that perplexes me.

On Saturday when I was at the Hollis's, a Mrs. Bessie Oliver came to see Dr. Dave. As soon as she came in the door, she cried out, "Oh woe is me, there's another diphtheria epidemic coming—I can feel it in my bones!" She was wringing her hands, and tears were streaming down her cheeks. Dr. Dave managed to calm her in his kind, reassuring manner. She soon went on her way again in a better frame of mind than when she had come.

Mrs. Dave explained to me how her troubles started nine years ago when the diphtheria epidemic went through. Her little three-year-old daughter died from it, and she has never really recovered from the shock. She's been neurotic ever since, filled with unreasonable fears and worries. Sometimes it's almost more than Dr. Dave can do to reassure and calm her. He said every spring when the Little Conemaugh River and the Stony Creek River run high from the snows melting off the mountains and the rains, she becomes hysterical, saying that the South Fork Dam is going to break, and the city of Johnstown will become flooded. To tell the truth, I've often thought about that great body of water, Lake Conemaugh, nestled between the mountains fourteen or so miles away. The lake is on a much higher elevation than Johnstown. I have wondered what would happen if the dam gave way. Papa has been up there, and he says the dam is around two hundred and seventy feet thick at the base and built of layers of clay and covered with huge rocks. Some were so big that it took three teams of horses to move them! Wow! That surely sounds as if it's substantially built. It's over nine hundred feet wide and rises seventy feet above the valley floor . . . Imagine! Besides, when the dam was built, a spillway was cut through the solid rock in the hillside where there is no danger of erosion to catch the overflow crashing down over boulders. So, I would imagine that the more it would rain, the more water would come down over the spillway, keeping the depths of the lake the same and keeping the water level from rising. At least, I hope so. But even so, it's kind of scary thinking about it sometimes. Every spring people talk about it, and even make jokes about the possibility of the dam breaking. I've heard say that it's the largest man-made lake in the country, but Papa says it isn't true. It's big though, approximately two and one half miles long and one mile wide. If you'd want to hike all around it, you'd have to walk five miles. The depth of it is sixty to seventy feet and the weight of it could be of up to twenty million tons! Whew! No wonder Mrs. Bessie Oliver gets scared. Actually, Papa says the dam did break once, in the spring of 1862. But not much happened because the lake was less than half full then, and the creeks were low at the time. There was a defect in the foundation of the dam. I suppose that would have been repaired then.

The lake has since been sold to a group of wealthy people for a hunting and fishing club. They probably would've done what was necessary to make it safe. I sure wouldn't mind seeing the lake. I've heard that it is very scenic. Vincent has offered to take Julie and me there sometime, but Papa says that it is private property and trespassers aren't welcome. Too bad.

Time to go, for I've just heard the sound of sleigh bells merrily ringing. Upon peeking out the window, I see Vincent come "flying" up the drive on the sleigh with his horse, Cavalier, snorting big puffs of steam in the frosty air.

January 4

Acause for rejoicing—Julie and I finally finished the quilts we've been working on all winter. Hers is a "Tumbling Block" pattern. Mine is a "Philadelphia Pavement." We had them in the big, round hoop frames in the east room. We helped each other a lot so we could finish together. They are beautiful—even if I do say so myself. It gives us a great feeling of accomplishment to have added another piece to our hope chests.

This afternoon we had a rather important caller, a Mr. Roscoe Eldridge. He is one of the top guys in the steel industry. Papa and Mama made his acquaintance a half year ago when his wife died of tuberculosis. He's in his mid thirties, quite well to do and high class. He has a lovely home on Prospect Hill with all the latest conveniences.

The reason for his coming here: He's looking for a helper to care for his little daughter. He also has two sons. He has stayed at home with the children since his wife died, making do with the help of his black cook and housekeeper, Chloe, the boys' tutor, the cleaning woman, the gardener and the butler. I'm just guessing now and probably exaggerating things, but now he's ready to go back to his job. So he needs a governess for five-year-old Iris. His boys are Patrick, thirteen, and Morgan, eleven. Someone recommended the Montgomery girls to him. So he arrived on our doorstep. Mama and Papa told him that they would talk it over with Julie and me and let him know soon. After he left, Mama called us into the library. We sat down to discuss the possibilities. Julie declared right away that she wants to be counted out; it doesn't sound the least bit appealing to her. I had to smile, for I knew that the real reason was she's hoping that Vincent will propose to her soon. And so they turned to me. I couldn't say that I wasn't interested because the idea intrigued me immensely. Its not every day that I'm offered a job I can do. With my lame leg, hard, strenuous work is out. Nor am I particularly fond of sewing (at least not for other people). I don't have any aptitude for being a Schoolmarm. Mama thinks it's a wonderful opportunity for me. I am inclined to be feeling the same way. Mr. Eldridge would pay excellent wages. It would broaden my horizons, and probably be very rewarding as well. He's coming back tomorrow for an answer, and if it is yes, I am to begin the job immediately.

I'm afraid I shall be too excited to sleep tonight. At least I'll have something pleasant and exciting to think about.

This has to be it for now. Pearl just came up with a stack of mending for me to do, and so I'll exchange my pen for a needle and thimble.

January 5

Vincent was just here. He and Julie went for a walk to the top of the knob behind the barn "to see the stars" as he put it. Well, well, I don't think he was particularly interested in the stars, even though they are quite magnificent. I had been out on a short stroll myself and, as always, was awed by the splendor of the millions of twinkling lights in the coal black sky, looking so clear and close that you almost think you could reach out and pluck one. But no, I don't think it was stargazing that drew them. When they came back later with rosy cheeks and glowing faces, Julie's eyes were positively shining. She didn't say a word, though, of what transpired out there, except to say that Vincent told her there's a tobogganing party in Ebensburg tomorrow night. He offered to take Julie and me on the sleigh. How very kind of him to include me, too, when I know being alone would mean a lot to them. Of course, I politely declined, but Julie was so adamant about it, insisting that I must go along. I finally said I would. Three's a crowd, the saying goes, but, oh well, maybe my own Prince Charming will come along in due time (one that doesn't mind a lame leg!). Until that happens I will be satisfied as I am. And, if it never does, I shall be a happy and cheerful old maid (I hope).

There are so many inventions and changes coming along, such as electricity, telephones, telegraph, and typewriters—it's hard to keep up with them all. We are coming into a glorious new age, according to Uncle Otto. Papa and Mama are reluctant to admit that some of these things are as glorious as they sound; they prefer to cling to the old ways. At any rate, there are a lot of golden opportunities all around us; the most important one being the opportunity of doing good unto others (my, don't I sound pious!). To tell the truth, I have my own interests that I'm so very fond of, such as my music and art. And yet, I have a desire to obey the Biblical injunction—whatever I do, do it heartily, as unto the Lord and to the honor and glory of God.

January 6

We just came back from the tobogganing party, and did we ever have heaps of fun! The ride to Ebensburg on the sleigh with Vincent was half the fun, whizzing through the cold, frosty air at a fast clip, with the millions of stars twinkling overhead. We met up with some more partygoers on sleighs. The air rang with the merry laughter of the girls, and the salutations of the boys. Vincent's horse, Cavalier, just wanted to race. We were fairly flying, his hooves barely skimming over the frozen crusts of snow. They're planning a skating party on the Von Lunen pond as soon as the weather creates ice right for it. They've been trying to clear the ice of its layers of snow, but it isn't very smooth. Maybe if we'd have a thaw, and then another hard freeze before it snows again, it would become clear as glass.

It always puts a pang in my heart when the others plan something that I can't participate in, even though I don't begrudge them their fun. I'll have to count the blessings I have, and there are many!

The tobogganing was so much fun, too, thanks to Vincent and Julie. They pulled me back up the hill each time. The hill was steep, the rides fast and exhilarating, like flying, and what they did for me was no mean task. I hope I can repay all that others have done for me, someday, but, if not, they'll surely have their reward in the hereafter.

And, oh yes, Roscoe Eldridge was here today. Our answer to him was in the affirmative. I can't help but feel excited about it, terribly excited. Monday will be my first day. I'm a mixture of trepidation and eager anticipation. I know I won't be able to sleep right away, so I think I'll put another log on the fire and curl up in bed with my new book, *Jo's Boys* by Louisa May Alcott. It's a sequel to *Little Women* and *Little Men*, and a good one. Goodnight!

I'm curled up on the big window seat in the library, with a cheery fire crackling on the hearth. The lights of Johnstown twinkle up at me. I want to write all about my day. I'll start out with describing Roscoe. Yes, he asked me to call him by his first name. He calls me Johanna rather than Miss Montgomery. He looks too young to be the father of a thirteen-year-old, even though he has twinges of gray at the temples; his features are almost boyish. He's good looking, and the gray gives him a touch of sophistication or distinction, but he can't compare to Vincent's handsome, honest-hearted friendliness. (Excuse my grammar.) Patrick and Morgan both look a lot like their dad, but little Iris does not. She's darker complected and tiny for her age, with big, wistful eyes. She talks with a lisp. She's the kind that you just want to scoop up into your arms the minute you see her and mother her properly. Then, there's the fat, roly-poly cook and housekeeper, Chloe, who's just like a member of the family. Her mother was a slave (before the war, of course) in the Eldridge household when Roscoe was a little boy. Chloe still talks like the old slaves did. I love to hear her talk; it's very quaint and charming. Her "honey child, and sho nuff and dem dar's" sound very dignified and proper, though, when she uses them. She's still a great worker, in spite of her age. Maybe she's not even so very old—it's hard to tell.

Next I'll describe the house. It's really elegant and has all the latest conveniences and inventions. There's indoor plumbing, an icebox, Brussels carpets in every room of the house except the kitchen, both a majestic organ, and a grand piano, open stairways, Arab scarves, and an ivory clock from Europe. There are ornately carved scrolls and polished woodwork. Drapes are of rich brocade; the height of luxury if you ask me—quite a contrast from our homely place with its worn furniture and lived in look. Even the barn is elegant for the driving horses and the cow.

There's a big pool and a splashing fountain out front—the biggest I've ever seen. Of course, it's not splashing now, in the middle of winter, but Patrick described to me how it is in the summertime. The lawn is huge, with lots of landscaping—shrubs trimmed into a variety of shapes and sizes, and lots of boxwood. The capping of snow on all the different bushes made them look quite regal and picturesque.

I think I must've guessed right about the servants in this household. Besides the boys' tutor, there are all the others I mentioned except a butler. I spent the morning entertaining Iris, reading to her for a while. Then she wanted to play in the snow so we bundled up and had a lively romp, and also went for a walk. Luckily, Aunt Rolla can't see me from here! Some things are worth having an aching leg for!

Iris is such a sweet, shy little thing. I know I'm going to love my new job! This afternoon while Iris was napping, Chloe put me to knitting a muff that matches her Sunday coat. Just before supper Roscoe came home and told me to bundle up—he was going to drive me home himself. Well I never!

Supper was ready when I came home, and Vincent was here for the meal. I mentioned how surprised I was that Roscoe hadn't gotten his coachman to drive me home instead of doing it himself. Papa said that Roscoe actually came from a poor family, and is probably still a country boy at heart. It was his wife that wanted to live surrounded by luxury. So that explains it.

Vincent stayed after supper to play a few games. We had a jolly evening, later popping popcorn over the fire, and roasting horse chestnuts. Julie brought a bowl of Northern Spy apples up from the cellar. Aunt Rolla and Uncle Otto dropped in, too. They told stories of long ago. Aunt Rolla told of the time when she was a little girl of eleven and just finished washing the breakfast dishes. She flung her dishpan full of dirty dishwater out the back door just as her grandfather came around the corner of the house. He got it full in the face! Her father was very provoked at her for being so careless. He made her sit alone in her room all the while Grandpa was there. This was a real punishment for her because his visits were very rare and special. He always brought hard candy. She was very hurt; she hadn't done it on purpose. Grandpa pitied her, too. Before he left he walked a block down to the General Store and bought a little round china dish with a lid. He filled it with hard candy and gave it to her. She has treasured it always. It still sits on the bureau in her bedroom.

Ho hum, I'm just yawning every minute. I can't keep my eyes open any longer—I guess it's because I finished *Jo's Boys* last night. I believe it was early morning rather than late before I was done. I suppose I should've made some New Year's resolutions!

January 11

*M*y third day at my new job has passed. I'm happy to say that I've loved every minute of it, so far. But now something has happened that has paled the new job almost into insignificance! We've had a letter from our step-cousin, Miss Meredith Montgomery, who lives in Philadelphia. Let me explain how she joined our extended family: Papa's brother Clay married a widow with a small daughter (Meredith). They gave her the name Montgomery, too, at that time. When Meredith was just a few years old she became an orphan when her mother and stepfather both died of consumption at the same time. She has lived with her aunt in Philadelphia ever since. Now her aunt has died, too. She's alone in the world, as she puts it. She found Papa's name and address in an old family Bible. She has asked in her letter if she can come and live with us. She's just about six months younger than I am, and six months older than Julie. At the time of Uncle Clay's death, Papa and Mama had tried to correspond with the aunt who was caring for little Meredith. They were severely rebuffed. They figured that probably the aunt was afraid they'd try to take the little girl away from her. So I guess that's why we never heard from her before now. We never even got to meet her.

Papa and Mama called a meeting in the library to talk it over. Even Pearl was present because taking in a boarder will affect her, too. The vote was unanimous that we can't turn her away or refuse to give her a home. Now it remains to be seen what she's like; a cheerful, fresh-faced country-at-heart-lass, or a hoity-toity city gal (smiles). It should prove to be interesting, almost like getting another sister in the family. Mama wrote her a letter tonight, saying she's welcome to come as soon as she pleases. Later, Julie and I sat in our room talking until late. We were about as excited as could be. There are so many new and exciting things happening lately! This world is so full of a number of scenes, I'm sure that we all should be happy as queens!

February 1

I've been neglecting you lately, dear journal. We've been so very busy. There's my new job at the Eldridge's. Then in the evenings I've been helping to get the "east room" as we call it, ready for Meredith. We've repainted the walls and the woodwork. We've varnished the hardwood floor, made new curtains for the windows. We put down the big rug that Pearl braided this winter out of strips of cloth from outgrown dresses, or the ragbag, as she calls it. Vincent helped, too, whenever he could. He's every bit as curious about the new girl as Julie and I. She's to arrive in a week. We can hardly wait! She will be traveling by train. I'll bet she's as excited about it as we. I had a train ride to Pittsburgh five years ago and thought it quite an experience! I've been trying to visualize what Meredith will look like, but my imagination fails me. I've nothing to go by, since she's not a blood relative of ours. Just one more week and I'll know.

February 4

Today was another worthwhile and rewarding Saturday spent with the Hollis's. The weather has turned milder. We had an all-day rain. So the snow is melting fast. As we had our cozy "tea" by the fire after the work was done, Dr. Dave launched into the subject of Lake Conemaugh—the South Fork dam. Whenever there's rain, people begin to talk about flooding here in Johnstown. He said that the lake is much deeper since the hunting and fishing club bought it and repaired the dam. They have stocked it with lots of fish. The grounds are well posted: No Hunting and Fishing Allowed. This is a big temptation for boys and even men in the neighborhood to sneak onto the property in the early morning or towards sundown when there's no one around to see them. The fishing is good and many a tasty supper is thus provided in the neighborhood. The club once put up fences to discourage this. The fences mysteriously disappeared. This prompted the club authorities to threaten to shoot any trespassers caught on the grounds after dark. Another interesting thing he told me was that in 1881 on the morning of June 10th there was a flash flood, and a rumor spread through Johnstown that the dam was about to break. This threw a terrific panic into the people as word spread from house to house and flew up one street and down the next, and across the alleys. But it was a false alarm—nothing of the sort happened. The sun set as usual. Dawn rolled around and life went on as it had previously. There really had been no cause for alarm. But just about every spring since then there have been rumors about the dam breaking. People ask why the dam wasn't somehow reinforced and strengthened. There's probably hardly a man or woman in Johnstown who at sometime or other hasn't had misgivings about that great body of water above them and spoken of the terrible catastrophe that could happen should the dam break. But now it appears as if their fears were groundless for nothing so terrible has ever happened. People still talk about it a lot, but it's mostly in the line of making jokes than anything else. According to Dr. Dave, it's becoming a local joke. Whenever there are rumors about the dam breaking, no one takes them to heart. Everyone's calloused to the possibility of danger. Perhaps there is no danger at all—the dam has always held so far. There was an article in the Tribune newspaper last year that said even though the South Fork dam should break, it would not greatly affect Johnstown unless it occurred at the same time as a great flood, and that's a possibility not worth mentioning. It's a comforting thought at any rate. It's no use becoming hysterical like Mrs. Bessie Oliver.

Dr. Dave talked about our need to be ready to meet our Maker, regardless of whether or not there's a danger of the dam breaking. Tomorrow is not promised to any of us. He then told me a pearl of a story that supposedly happened during the eruptions of the volcano Vesuvius, in the last days of Pompeii. There was a blind girl, Nydia, living there. She had not become bitter about the fact that she was blind and others could see but had cheerfully accepted her handicap. Instead of sulking and sitting at home, she had gone about her business of living her life to the fullest. Then, when the awful day of Vesuvius' eruption, and the city of Pompeii was doomed to destruction, she put the handicap to good use. A thick pall of smoke and falling ashes made everything as pitch dark as midnight. The terror stricken inhabitants of the city rushed blindly to and fro, trying to escape before they were buried alive under lava. But being confused and not knowing which way to turn, they got lost in the awful blackness. But Nydia didn't get lost because of her cross of blindness. She had learned to find her way by touch and hearing. She could rescue the lives of the ones she loved best. By learning to walk swiftly and surely in the dark she had made of her handicap a treasure and a Godsend in the dark hour.

Dr. Dave then went on to say that God has the power to transform every misfortune, failure and loss in our lives into blessings. Out of life's hard knocks may come our richest reward. And, Mrs. Dave added, with a twinkle in her eyes, "No wound, no pearl!"

The rain had stopped when I began my walk home, but almost as soon as I was on the street, it began to drizzle. My leg was aching, and I wondered how God was going to transform my handicap into a blessing. At that moment I heard the staccato of horses' hooves coming from behind. The jolly voice of Vincent called out, "Ho, Johanna, hop on, and be nimble and quick about it!" I didn't need to be invited twice! He had Papa's span of horses hitched, and I was whisked home in a jiffy.

I do have a lot of blessings—more than I deserve. I want to always be thankful and grateful for them. Time for bed, for tomorrow is Sunday and we have church services. Just three more days and Meredith will be here. Meredith Montgomery—how poetic that sounds. I can hardly wait.

Roscoe Eldridge gave me a half-day off, so I could be here when Meredith arrives. She came on the noon train. Papa and Mama met her at the station with the horses and carriage. My first impression of her was Wow! How stunning! With her beautifully coiffed honey-colored hair and striking gray eyes, and her elegant apparel, she reminded me of an actress on a stage. She refused dinner, saying she had a headache. She asked to be shown to her room and stayed there until suppertime. I met Julie in the hall. She whispered, "Doesn't she seem kind of cold and haughty?" I shushed her, asking her how sociable she felt when she had a splitting headache. We'd invited Aunt Rolla, Uncle Otto, and Vincent for supper, so they could meet Meredith. We were almost afraid she wouldn't show up at the table. At the last minute she "swept" into the room in a beautiful long dress of pale green. Dark green sprigs were throughout, with shimmering lace at the neckline and cuffs of her voluminous sleeves. I don't know what she'd done, but her coiffed hair seemed more magnificent than ever. Her eyes were more luminously striking. Vincent's usual ready wit was struck dumb, or so it seemed to me. Perhaps he was totally mesmerized by the lovely lady. (Smiles). But, if Meredith had seemed "cold and haughty" when she arrived, she was just the opposite at the supper table. I'm not exaggerating— she could have charmed the birds off their nests! And she flirted outrageously with Vincent, who had recovered his composure by then, and reciprocated in kind. Julie seemed quiet and subdued throughout the meal. I know just how she felt. This was "our" Vincent Meredith was flirting with . . . and he seemed to like it! Even Pearl was disturbed by the goings-on. She kept casting dark looks at "Miss Meredith," as she calls her, and muttering unintelligible phrases under her breath as she served the oyster stew. Aunt Rolla, who was seated at my right, was quieter than usual. I'm not sure I heard right, but once I thought I heard her hissing under her breath the words, "the hussy." She was sipping coffee—it sounded little more than a soft sigh. In all my wildest imaginings I never once dreamed of Meredith being like this! I feel vaguely disturbed—like we're on the verge of something unsettling happening.

My eyes seem to catch the verse on the homemade motto on the wall: Take It To The Lord In Prayer. I feel the need of doing just that right now. It's comforting to know that we can take all our "cares perplexing" to the heavenly Father and let Him solve our problems. Goodnight.

February 29 Leap Year's Day

*M*y mother's thirteenth birthday! Whew! Doesn't that sound ridiculous! Actually it's her fifty-second birthday. Because she was born on Leap Year's

Day, in 1836, she has had only thirteen birthdays to call her own. Papa celebrated the day by taking her to the downtown hotel for supper and a concert afterwards. After all, she's had only seven birthdays since they've married. I knitted her a scarf. Julie made her a set of handkerchiefs with lovely crocheted edgings for her birthday gift. Mother thanked us sincerely, with shining eyes, for the gifts and for being loving, obedient and satisfying daughters (her own words). She's truly a noble and gracious woman.

We are getting used to having Meredith in our household. I won't write that we are exactly delighted she's here. I don't mean to be critical and complaining, but surely, dear journal, you won't repeat to anyone else what I write, nor spread gossip. I don't like to say she's two-faced, but what else could you call it? Whenever Vincent is around (and he seems to be around more than ever since she came) she is as bright, charming, gay and witty as anyone I've ever seen, but to the rest of us she's not. Julie said tonight she could almost grind her teeth in rage when she sees Meredith (I never have thought Julie could get that upset) smiling at Vincent in that loving, almost intimate way of hers, and him smiling back. I tried to tell her that Vincent is too smart to fall for Meredith's put on charms, but now I, too, have a hard time convincing myself that he doesn't think her an ever-so-sweet little lady. It disturbs me to no end to see Julie withdraw, pale and quiet when Meredith begins to flaunt her cunning wiles.

The other night at the supper table Meredith created quite a "little scene" when the stew Pearl served was not quite to her liking. Papa quietly reprimanded her (just as he used to reprimand us girls when we complained about the food on the table). Apparently it doesn't take much to insult her. She flounced off upstairs to her room in a huff. Now, if Vincent had been here, she'd have been jolly and laughing—completely the opposite. I have a good notion to tell him how different she is when he's not here. I said as much to Mama. She shook her head, and with that serene smile of hers, said that he will see soon enough just how shallow she is. I must say that I'm very surprised and disappointed that he seems to be so taken in by her. I suppose if I saw only the one side of her, I'd be fooled, too. I'd think her the sweetest most gracious, and most stunningly beautiful young woman I'd ever seen. Poor Vincent has a jolt coming to him. Let's hope it's soon, before he is hurt (and Julie, too).

Thanks, journal, for permitting me to let off steam. Perhaps it's not half as bad as I make it out to be, and I'm just magnifying things because I can't stand to see Julie suffer. I hope and pray it is so.

March 8

Spring will be here in a few weeks. It was not hard to believe today. The air was warm and balmy. I heard a robin chirping. Pussy willows will soon be blooming. The mountains will be greening up again, and the flowers blooming. When Roscoe brought me home tonight (in the two-wheeled cart with a saddle bred horse hitched), he spoke of planting more fruit trees this spring, putting a kitchen garden out back, and flower garden in the front yard. Of course, he wouldn't think of doing all this if he hadn't a gardener ready to do his bidding. I think it must be wonderful to be rich. Papa doesn't quite agree with me. We could be quite a bit more "well-to-do" if he wouldn't give so much to help the poor and less fortunate than ourselves. He doesn't believe in living a rich man's life—he says that no matter how heavily we are endowed with this world's goods or how big an income we have, we should live in simple, common homes, wear plain and modest clothes, live frugally, and then give what we can to the less fortunate. By our way of living, no one should suspect wealth. Hmmmm . . . it makes sense, according to the Bible. But it would be lovely to dress in expensive, elegant clothes, dine on rich and exotic foods, live in grand homes and be surrounded with all the luxuries and comforts available, and travel to faraway places to see all the wonders of the world.

Roscoe has quite a lot to say to me lately on our drives. I am beginning to feel like one of the family the way he includes me in plans for the children. He says he wants to take us all on a picnic to Lake Conemaugh sometime this spring when the weather becomes favorable. He has a friend who works for the South Fork Hunting and Fishing Club, a private summer resort. Through him he's going to get us the permission. He's thinking of becoming a member of the club himself sometime, but will postpone it for a while. I sure look forward to going. I've heard so much about that big lake and dam. I'd like to see it myself. He knows a lot about the history of Johnstown, too.

The first white settlers in the valley were Solomon and Samuel Adams, and their sister Rachael, who came over the Allegheny Mountains from Bedford in 1771 and cleared a patch of land near the Stony Creek River. The Indians killed Samuel and Rachael. Solomon wasted no time in returning to Bedford. It was another twenty years before the next permanent settler arrived—Joseph Schantz, or Johns, an Amish farmer, with his wife and four children (that's where the name Johnstown came from). He cleared off thirty acres between the rivers, built a cabin, planted an orchard, and laid out a village, which he first called Old Conemaugh Town. He moved out later, but the village continued to prosper. By 1840 there was a population of around three thousand people, and the name had been changed to Johnstown. It's hard to believe, but Roscoe says that today there's a population of close to thirty thousand people! I asked him why the big reservoir (Lake Conemaugh) was ever made in the first place. He explained that it was to supply water for the canal system from Johnstown to Pittsburgh during the dry months in the summer. The dam was completed in 1852. It had cost $240,000 to build. Then just two years later it was obsolete and of no use whatsoever; the Pennsylvania railroad came through and the canals weren't used anymore. There was, by then, a daring rail route over the mountains, including the famous Horseshoe Curve. After that, nothing whatsoever was done to maintain the dam. Nine years ago in 1879 the South Fork Hunting and Fishing Club bought it. Still it was left alone, quietly moldering away in the woods, visited only once in a while by fishermen or deer hunters. When the club bought it, the dam held little more than a pond because of the break in 1862. It was ten feet deep at the deepest point, with grass growing over acres and acres of dried up lakebed. They repaired the dam to its former level. Today the lake is sixty to seventy feet deep and covers four hundred and fifty acres. The water comes from half a dozen streams and little creeks that rush down from the Blue Knob and Allegheny Mountains. Cottages and clubhouses now surround the lake. The South Fork Hunting and Fishing Club has a thriving business going with over sixty members. The membership fee is $800. So, it's only for the rich and elite. I consider myself fortunate that I'll be getting a chance to see it. Roscoe said there are sailboats on the lake—an unheard of thing in this part of the country. I hope the weather continues to warm up fast, so we can go soon.

Oh, oh. I've got to go. Pearl's calling me—she's promised to teach me the art of making cream puffs. I heard her riddling down the ashes on the big cook stove in the kitchen a while ago. I guess the stove is hot enough now. But, I suppose things will never be the same again (sigh); at least not as long as Meredith is here. In the evenings Vincent used to come in and sample the delicacies Julie and I made, and perhaps help with the dishes. We'd have a jolly time together. Now there's always Meredith making eyes at him and hogging all the attention. Julie is hurting. My heart aches for her. I don't really for a minute believe that Vincent will ever become seriously interested in a flapper like Meredith.

PART TWO
Joys and Shadows

*L*ittle Iris is such a sweet, winsome child. At least several times a day she comes to me and throws her arms around me, saying, "I wish you'd be my Mama." Imagine that! I've seen a photograph of her mother. What a great and fashionable lady she must've been; the belle of every party, the mistress of a rich man's home. I just hug the child back and tell her I'll be a big sister to her instead.

Roscoe has bought a pony and cart for Patrick and Morgan. It's "all the rage" for them just now. They're quite willing to give rides to Iris and me. The pony is so gentle they've let Iris drive for a few turns around the carriage shed. Poor Chloe became so agitated when she saw it. She came outside, rolling her eyes and wringing her hands—Patrick said afterward that she fluttered like a hen when its brood of chicks is disturbed. He said she shook her finger at him, saying, "I declar', Mas'r Patrick, you must be addled in the head, mor's de pity," (in exact imitation of her.) She is like a conscientious mother hen, brooding over her chicks. She goes to prayer meeting twice a week, and she says she "rassles in pra'r" for her motherless little lambs.

These past few weeks, Chloe has been in a siege of housecleaning. I'm helping her, in spite of her shaking her finger at me, and saying, "I declar', Miss Josie, (her pet name for me) you don' need to help ole Chloe—no use getting dem pretty white hands soiled." She wears an old turban on her head when she cleans. She says everything must have a regular overhaulin' or "clarin' up." The carpets must be taken up and "walloped." All the curtains washed. She gathers up all the brooms, brushes and mops and makes the dust fly. She scrubs until the soapsuds fly and every bone in her body aches. After the parlor had its regular overhaulin' (wid de carpets up and whaled, and de furniture turned out of do'ahs to air), she complained that she "cotched a misery in her back and laigs dat was worsen' de rheumatiz." Her knees were stiff. She cleans with a vengeance, and when I offer to do something she's doing, she says, "mercy no, chile, yo take keer o' dat lame laig." She's a dear old soul, and every bit as beloved in their household as our "Pearl of great price" is in ours. I'm getting to be just as attached to her as I am to Pearl.

April 1

"Beside them the birds of heaven nest, among the branches they sing." Psalm 104:12. Spring is truly here. The time of the singing of the birds is come. Today was a lovely Sunday, mild, with abundant sunshine. We heard an inspiring sermon at church, entitled "Surveying The Cross." Afterward we got a delicious dinner at Aunt Rolla and Uncle Otto's. After dinner Vincent came around with Cavalier hitched to the buggy. The minute Meredith saw him, she jumped up and skipped out the door. Her peal of merry laughter floated back to us as they drove off together. The downcast look on Julie's face was heart-rending. It took the sunshine out of the day for us, for a while. But, as Papa said, "It is all in God's hands." Julie and I went out walking. We soon almost forgot our troubles about Vincent and Meredith. There's so much to see in Johnstown on a lovely Sunday afternoon. Lots of families were out walking, dressed in their Sunday best. We greeted most all of them, and spoke a few words with all we knew. Someone has described our coal and steel town as "new, rough, and busy," with the rush of the huge mills and factories and the throb of perpetually passing trains. The Cambria Iron Company has its giant three-ton converters going night and day, making steel for rails, barbed wire, plowshares, track bolts, and spring teeth harrows. The valley is often full of smoke during working hours. The entire city clanks, whistles, and rumbles loud enough to be heard for miles around. At night the sky gleams red from the furnaces. A visitor has once remarked that it appears as if the whole valley were on fire—a sure sign of prosperity, he called it.

Patrick and Morgan Eldridge came by, driving their father's saddle bred horse hitched to the spring wagon. They offered to take us along to the Unique Roller Skating Rink. My leg was aching by that time. So we hopped on the back and rode in style. We watched them skating for a while, then headed for the river. A fine, new carriage passed us, drawn by a span of high-headed horses. A handsome young man was driving. Patrick said it was Thomas Layton, an acquaintance of his dad's. He was an employee at the South Fork Hunting and Fishing Club. I believe he's the one who will get us the permission to picnic there.

We spotted an eagle flying high overhead above the mountains. Johnstown is really kind of down in a hole. Rather, it just seems that way because of the mountains. A visitor once remarked that here, the sun rises at ten and sets at two, which is an exaggeration. All around there are densely forested ridges (hogbacks, they are called) rolling off in every direction like a turbulent green sea. Papa has hiked to the top in his younger years. He says it takes the breath right out of you. Up there it's like another world, clean, open, and sweet smelling. The rivers are running high just now, with the Little Conemaugh, which is much the swifter of the two, rushing in from the east, and the Stony Creek, which is broader and deeper, flowing in from the south. They meet at Johnstown, forming the Conemaugh River, which farther west joins the Loyalhanna to form the Kiskiminetas. It in turn flows into the Allegheny about eighteen miles above Pittsburgh. I love to see the rivers when they're high, like they usually are this time of year. And year round, the fishing is superb.

Roscoe talks of taking the whole family on a fishing trip soon. He's also an avid hunter. He says that the geese, pheasants, ruffed grouse, and wild turkeys are still plentiful in the mountains. There are a few big gobblers around that weigh twenty pounds each. West of town on Laurel Hill there are still deer, black bears and wildcats.

Papa remembers (when he was a boy) of there being panthers in the mountains big enough to carry off a whole sheep. All in all, Johnstown, in spite of its drawbacks, is a wonderful place to live. Of course, there is the seamier side of it, too, such as the saloons and the tramps. Then there are also the drifters who come with the railroad looking for jobs and sometimes heading west toward Pittsburgh. But no matter how many come, it seems they can all find jobs if that is what they want. It seems like every day a couple of tramps or drifters come knocking on the back door for something to eat. Papa has instructed Pearl to never turn anyone away hungry. We stayed so long at the river, enjoying the scenery that Roscoe came riding down on horseback to see where the boys were so long. He said that Chloe is so worried that she's wringing her hands and 'rasslin' in pra'r, the poor soul. They all left posthaste, dropping Julie and me off at Uncle Otto's. It was a day well spent, and ended on a happy note because Vincent came over in the evening, probably to make amends for having run off with Meredith this afternoon. She had gone to her room as soon as Vincent brought her home. She refused to come down for supper. I wanted in the worst way to ask Vincent what had happened, but didn't dare. I hope they had a fall-out, and a serious enough one to be permanent. Vincent seemed like his usual self, jolly and lots of fun. It seemed like our old merry times, playing checkers with him, one game after another, the library ringing with laughter. Praise the Lord.

April 4

here's a chorus of robins, song sparrows, and turtledoves singing and cooing tonight. The grass in the orchard is getting to be a lovely shade of green. Papa decided that it's fit to plant our garden tonight after supper. We all pitched in to help. Meredith hasn't really been herself since Sunday. There was a rather cold, hard expression on her pretty face, and a cynical look about her mouth most of the time. Mama asked her if she wanted to help plant the garden, but she declined, saying disdainfully that such grubby work was beneath her. We had just begun to make the rows when Vincent showed up and offered to help. It was the first time he came since Sunday. Well, dear journal, let me tell you, just what happened then. The back door opened, and here came Meredith, all smiles and the soul of loveliness, wanting to help, too. It made Julie sputter a bit, but we all held our peace. She worked alongside Vincent, holding the seed bag for him, and chattering away at a great rate. Soon they were both laughing gaily. Meredith was flirting again—flirting outrageously, teasing and joking prettily. Pearl kept casting dark looks her way and muttering things not lawful to be uttered under her breath. So, I guess if Vincent and Meredith had quarreled, they must've made up again. "Mor's de pity" as Chloe would say. When I passed Pearl to get the hoe, she said in a loud whisper, "She's just like those 'daughters of Zion' you read about in Isaiah, who walk with stretched forth necks and wanton eyes, walking and mincing as they go, and making a tinkling with their feet." I couldn't help giggling at her comparison. I saw Meredith turn just then, and give me a hard look. Dear journal, I think I'm exaggerating these things to you.

I hope Meredith really isn't as bad as I make her sound. It's just that my heart is so sore for Julie's sake. It's a comfort for me to put her down. I did so want to have Vincent for a brother-in-law. Oh well, I guess I'll just have to trust all things will work together for good for all of us. Anyway, we got the garden planted, and it's a good thing we did because all signs point to rain tomorrow. Let it rain—the peas, onions, carrots, red beets, potatoes and lettuce seeds are all in the ground, waiting for moisture so they can grow. And I'm going to turn over a new leaf: I'm resolved to never again "put down" Meredith here in my journal. I'll look to her better side and mention only the good about her, if I mention her at all. Goodnight, dear journal.

*Y*ou poor old journal, I've been sadly neglecting you of late, but my life has just been so full and busy. On Friday night Roscoe asked me to go along to the Washington Street Show to see "Uncle Tom's Cabin." I figured it was to be another family outing, so of course my answer was yes. But I was wrong—it was just him and me alone, wonder of wonders! But maybe I'm being silly and reading something into his asking me that isn't there at all. The show was really something to see. They featured a pack of genuine bloodhounds trailing the runaway slaves. It all seemed so real and authentic. It has been said that the author of *Uncle Tom's Cabin* (Harriet Beecher Stowe) is the little woman that started the big war. It was quite a drama—Topsy, Simon Legree, and all the rest.

And now yesterday we've had our fishing trip to Stony Creek. That definitely was a family affair—a real treat for the boys. They made out well at fishing: pulling out trout, catfish, mullet, sunfish, and wall-eyed pike, one after the other. Morgan even hooked a writhing eel. Iris screamed in terror and clung to me, as if she feared it might strangle her like a Cobra. So he threw it back. We had a wonderful day! Weather wise, it was warm as summer. The sky was the bluest of blue, with white clouds floating here and there. The birds were trilling joyously. The river water was clear and sparkling, flowing between the sun-bleached boulders on the riverbed. Downstream from town the river is stained by waste dumped from the mills. But where we were, it seemed to be crystal clear. We spread our blankets on the bank, and set out the feast Chloe had packed: a whole roast chicken, freshly baked bread, a jar of strawberry preserves, cubes of her delicious homemade cheddar cheese, a dried apple pie, a peach dessert and raisin filled cookies.

After dinner Roscoe and the boys went on a hike. Iris and I sat on the riverbank barefoot, dipping our toes into the water. Iris stared thoughtfully at my leg, and then asked me why I am lame. I mumbled something about supposing it must be God's will, and then she asked, "If Jesus were here right now, could He make your leg well?" I assured her that indeed He could, and someday He would do so, if not in this life, then in the next. She then asked a lot of questions about where her Mama is right now, and could she look down from Heaven and see us, and would she ever see her again, etc. I decided then and there that on Saturday at the Hollis's I would ask Dr. Dave about some of these things, so I can give her more satisfactory answers. After a moment of silence, she wistfully said, "I wish you could be my Mama now." Dear, sweet child. I hugged her and told her again that I would be a "big sister" to her. We could do a lot of "happy" things together. Thankfully, that seemed to satisfy her. What more could I have said to her?

I've heard it being said that there's nothing so kingly as kindness, and nothing so royal as truth. Julie and I had a long talk on Sunday evening (about Meredith) and decided that we have been as much at fault as she. We've failed to be kind to her, and she has reciprocated in kind. What set it off was the way she flirted with, and monopolized Vincent the very first evening she was here. It just disgusted and maddened us so. We were so vexed; he seemed to be smitten by her charms so much, that we gave her the cold shoulder treatment, which really was very unchristian of us. We never really gave her a chance—a chance to see if she would respond to unconditional love, kindness and acceptance. After all, Jesus instructed his followers to "return good for evil," to be kind, tenderhearted, forgiving one another, loving one another, and said "whatsoever ye do unto the least of these my brethren, ye do it unto me." We confessed our sins to each other and to God. We resolved to treat Meredith very kindly and lovingly after this. It will be interesting to see how she will respond. Dr. Dave once said to me that the people who deserve love the least need it the most. We felt that we should apologize to her, but she was gadding about so much that we didn't get the chance until last night, when we asked her to go for a walk with us. Surprisingly, she accepted.

We strolled out into the enchanting orchard, where the robins were joyously singing, and the sweet smelling pink and white apple blossoms were floating down on the evening breezes. The loveliness of the evening softened our moods. We were feeling quite mellow as we confessed our uncharitableness to her, and our desire to do better. She was visibly moved. Drawing her handkerchief out of her bosom, she began to wipe the tears away that filled her big gray eyes. She told us how mean and bad she'd been feeling lately, and how hurt she was that she didn't feel welcome in our home. Her confessions did much to soften our feelings toward her.

We began to talk in earnest. She told us about the aunt who brought her up. What she told us about her shed some light on the development of her own character. What a coldhearted, selfish woman her aunt must have been! When Meredith was seven years old, a friend gave her a kitten. It was the first thing she ever had that she could call her own. How dearly she loved that kitten! Her aunt was jealous (Meredith later realized). One morning the kitten had simply disappeared. A few years later Meredith adopted a stray puppy. The same thing happened—when the aunt saw how fond she was of the dog, it, too, mysteriously died (she later learned that her aunt had poisoned it). How the little girl wept and grieved! But soon after that she found a bosom friend—the first real friend she ever had. It was the girl in the house next door. They were the same age, and soon became inseparable. Once again the spiteful old aunt stepped in; she forbade them to continue the friendship. In fact, she strictly forbade them to ever see each other again. When Meredith ignored her aunt's threats and willfully disobeyed, she sold the house and they moved away. All the while, bitterness and rebellion were growing in Meredith's heart.

When she was sixteen, she and a young man, three years older, fell in love. Knowing how this would affect her aunt, Meredith kept it a secret from her. The young couple made plans to run away to be married. But somehow, her aunt found out about it, and immediately, in her own way, put a stop to it. When the young man suddenly, without a word of explanation, stopped coming to their designated meeting place, Meredith grew suspicious. She went to the boarding house where her beau was staying, and asked for him. The landlord told her that he had gone out west and would not be back. Meredith said she was filled with a boiling rage. She knew her aunt had to be behind his going. And so it was.

Just before she died the aunt confessed to Meredith that she had written the young man a letter (and signed Meredith's name) saying she never wanted to see him again. Since we know all this it will be easier for us to overlook our cousin's character flaws, and be kind to her. (But it still won't make it any easier seeing her wrap Vincent around her little finger). I have wished a thousand times that Meredith had not come to live with us. I still do, but from now on I'm going to make the best of the situation. I will treat her as royally as a queen, no matter how difficult it is. At least I'm going to try, and hope that God will be merciful and forgive me if I fail.

Oh, oh. I just heard the sound of hoof beats out front, and there's Vincent with Cavalier hitched to the cart. How I wish it were Julie running out to him instead of Meredith!

/May 10

*W*hat a chilly, rainy week this has been. The rain's still coming down in torrents. After supper I took our big umbrella, and "dashed" as fast as my lame leg would allow, down to Paxton's store for a spool of thread. A few old-timers were seated around the potbelly stove, exchanging tidbits of news, probably glad for a warm, dry place to pass the time, out of the rain. Old Mr. Benner, who is in his eighties, cackled, "Well now, this might just be the night the old dam is going to break," and the others all laughed. Someone else said, "The dam's supposed to break every year, but so far, it hasn't been very co-operative." And another one said, "Sometime the dam will give way, but it probably won't happen in our time." And Mr. Paxton, the storekeeper, said, "Joking aside, I was just down by the river to make a delivery. If the water rises any more, it will be in the streets. I tell you, the flooding in the spring gets worse every year—with the valley crowding up the way it is; the lumber and land more in demand every year. The trees are being stripped off the mountains and hills for lumber for building. Here in Johnstown the river channels are narrowed to make room for building, and, in several places, make it easier to put new bridges across. I declare . . . it's a crying shame," he added forcefully.

Mr. Benner cut in with, "I guess none of you here are old enough to remember the pumpkin flood that hit in the fall of 1820. It swept just about every pumpkin in Cambria County down into town—you'd have to have seen it to believe it. And we all remember the flood of 1847 when the dam on the Strong Creek broke. But that was nothing compared to what it was when the Cambria Iron dam went down eight years ago. That one was sixteen feet high. It was located below town, so no damage was done." Mr. Paxton muttered something about even that being a drop in the bucket compared to what it would be like should the big South Fork dam go, (which is over nine hundred feet wide and seventy two feet above the valley floor). I was tired of hearing about floods, and the rain seemed to be coming down faster than ever. I spent some time browsing around the store looking at all the merchandise—barrels of sugar and flour, tins of crackers, cases of ivory-colored laundry soap, Ewarts cigars, chewing tobacco, pickles in brine, queens ware, needles and thread, Clark's O.N.T. (our new thread), pins, and bolts of cloth.

The rain was drumming on the roof. I was beginning to think I'd been very foolish to venture out into the rain, when who should come in the door but Aunt Rolla and Uncle Otto. And, just as I figured, Aunt Rolla literally pounced on me like a mother hen. She was soon sending Uncle Otto posthaste to hitch Dobbin to the top buggy to take me home. I was feeling more foolish than ever. Aunt Rolla has a heart of gold, but she overdoes it sometimes with her protectiveness. Oh well, she has neither chick nor child of her own to mother. So she takes it out on her sister's daughters.

A merry, crackling fire in the fireplace in my room feels good again tonight. If the rain keeps up there certainly will be high water by tomorrow morning; maybe even flooding in the lowest streets. But, I guess that's just a price this town has to pay for living so close to these scenic rivers. Pearl (bless her heart) was just in, bringing me a mug of hot chocolate. Now it's time to head up for my cozy bed. It seems all the cozier with the rain pouring down.

May 11

Still raining. There's water in the streets below. Poor Chloe was very nervous about the high water, even though the Eldridge house is high and dry on Prospect Hill. She spent the afternoon wringing her hands, and 'rasslin' in pra'r for the poor folks "dat is likely to be drownded." Roscoe brought me home in style with his span of fine horses hitched to the spring wagon. We made a detour downtown to see how high the water really is. I asked him if there is a real danger of the South Fork dam giving way. He replied by telling me that several years ago the Cambria Iron Company sent two of its men to Lake Conemaugh with instructions to make a critical examination of the dam. The Johnstown men returned home with the report that the dam, or embankment appeared to be perfectly safe to stand all the pressure that can be brought to bear on it. They do not consider there is much cause for alarm, as even in the event of the dam breaking, there is plenty of room for the water to spread out before traveling the fourteen to fifteen miles to Johnstown, and no damage of moment should result. But others remained a little dubious about the matter. So the yearly talks about the dam breaking continue. At any rate, it's certainly nothing new to have water in the streets. Almost every spring we have some flooding, but there doesn't seem to be any cause for excitement.

Practically every spring there are rumors and warnings out about the dam breaking, but few take them to heart. Today down on the lower streets, people in raincoats were bailing water out of their cellars, and trying to move belongings off the first floor into the upstairs. A few children splashed about in the streets with wooden boxes, boards, or anything they could make a boat out of. The rivers were a muddy brown torrent. Every now and then a big piece of driftwood or a huge log came bounding along, as if on a mad race.

It was awesome to see. It sure made a person feel small and insignificant alongside such power. On the way back we met Judge McClarron sloshing along, carrying an umbrella and wearing overshoes. In a joking way, Roscoe asked him how much higher he thought the rivers would rise if the big dam broke. He studied for a moment, then replied, "High enough to wash out every bridge between here and there."

The horses ploughed right through the water in the streets with no fear—I guess because all their lives, or ever since they were colts, they've been used to it. When we drew up to our house, Roscoe said, almost tenderly, "Now sleep well tonight and don't worry about the dam breaking." And I shot back gaily, in a joking way, "It will be the least of my worries." Now I'm already repenting of what I said. Papa just came in tonight, and said there's a near—panic sweeping through the west end of town. Some people are in mortal dread for fear the dam won't hold. He said there are many in town living in sin, and not prepared to die. The dark and drenching rain unsettles their imaginations and fills them with the terror of death. He thinks it would be a good time to hold revival meetings, a much better time than when the sun is shining and "life is flowing along like a song."

God moves in a mysterious way
His wonders to perform.
He plants His footsteps in the sea
And rides upon the storm.

A beautiful day, sunny and so clear that it makes the hills seem even closer. The world seems so fresh and sparklingly clean after the rains. The grass is lush and green, the orchard yellow with dainty buttercups. Our sermon at church today was "Rescue The Perishing"—about reaching out to the many souls today who are caught by the raging floods of sin and swept away to eternal doom. While the panic of last week's mini-flood is over and life in Johnstown goes on as usual, we were warned that the flood tide of sin is a far greater danger. Satan is seeking to sweep away those who fail to "watch and pray," and are lulled into complacency.

This afternoon a group of teen-aged and older youths from church went to sing for the elderly and ailing. They all appreciated it immensely. Meredith, who has a good voice for singing, participated.

Dear journal, I have something good to write about Meredith (really and truly). She seems to be trying to be less self-centered, and that's saying a lot. But she still longs for the "good and easy" life (or, a rich man's life) I suppose, more of the world's "good things" and luxuries. She is appalled at how much Mama and Papa give to the poor, and how much better our standard of living could be if they saved it for themselves.

Tonight she came downstairs with her hair shining and beautifully upswept. She was wearing a pale lavender, softly clinging dress with a full, sweeping skirt. Her evening wrap matched her dusky eyes. She flashed us a dazzling smile and with a wave of her hand was out the door and climbing into Vincent's buggy. Cavalier was off with a bound. I don't blame Vincent for finding her irresistible, but, well . . . poor Julie. She excused herself and went to her room. My heart ached unbearably for her.

Later I was surprised to hear the rattle of wheels and hoof beats on the drive again. Roscoe was pulling up to the hitching post. Papa stepped outside to speak a few words to him, and soon came back inside, saying he had asked permission to take his daughter for a drive, if she was willing. His eyes were a mixture of twinkling and concern. When I came back an hour later, he confronted me in the hall, and wondered how long this has been going on. I told him that there's really nothing going on. It's nearly a year since Mrs. Eldridge died, and I suppose if he wanted to take a girl for a drive, it was his business. There was a look on Papa's face that told me he thought I was being childish and saucy, but I don't care. He probably thinks Roscoe a wealthy man of the world, but he isn't really. He's a church member and a devoted father to his children. And really, I don't think that just because he came to take me for a drive on a Sunday evening means anything significant. When he's ready to take a wife again, he will probably go for a fashionable society belle closer to his own age.

No matter what happens, I'd like to stay friends with Iris always, and be the big sister I promised. She's such a dear.

*A*nother rewarding day spent at the Hollis's. Mrs. Dave and I cleaned out the attic, and found a lot of old treasures. (Smiles). Out of an old book I copied an article entitled "The Bride." It was the story of a tribe of North American Indians who roamed in the neighborhood of Niagara Falls. Once a year they offered a young virgin as a sacrifice to the spirit of the mighty river. She was called "The Bride of the Falls." The lot fell one year on a beautiful girl who was the only daughter of an old chieftain. The news was carried to him while he was sitting in his tent. On hearing it, the old man went on smoking his pipe, and said nothing of what he felt.

On the day fixed for the sacrifice, a white canoe, full of ripe fruits, and decked with beautiful flowers, was ready, waiting to receive "The Bride."

At the appointed hour she took her place in the frail bark, which was pushed out into mid-stream, where it would be carried swiftly toward the mighty cataract.

Then, to the amazement of the crowd assembled to watch the sacrifice, a second canoe was seen to dart out from the river's bank a little lower down the stream. In it was seated the old chieftain.

With swift strokes he paddled towards the canoe in which was his beloved child. Upon reaching it, he gripped it firmly and held fast. The eyes of both met in one last long look of love, and then, close together, the racing current carried father and daughter until they plunged over the thundering cataract, and perished side by side.

In their death they were not divided. The father was "in it" with the child. So also, God was in Christ, reconciling the world unto Himself. He did not have to. Nobody forced Him. The only force behind the sacrifice was the force of His seeking love for the lost world, Author Unknown.

But there is a difference: Instead of merely perishing with lost humanity, Jesus was victorious over death. He rose again, and is able to save to the uttermost all who come to Him.

June 6

*A*t last we've had our long awaited picnic day at Lake Conemaugh. Chloe packed us a sumptuous feast. They all piled into Roscoe's spring wagon, with the coachman driving and came over here and picked me up. It was so early in the morning that the sun was just beginning to rise, casting its morning rays over the fresh, dewy, misty landscape. It was a nice cool morning, just the lovely weather we had all hoped it would be. The coachman dropped us off at the station. I think I was as excited as the children were when we boarded the train. It was so very interesting—the entire clang and clack, the long drawn out whistle, and seeing the surrounding countryside go by.

When we alighted at South Fork, which is the town closest to the lake, we rented a spring wagon with two well-matched, high-headed horses to take us the rest of the way. Going through South Fork, dogs burst out barking, and curious children stood watching us drive by. When we waved to them, they smiled and waved back. In two weeks when the summer season starts at the lake, it will be a common sight for them to see people coming and going; mostly well-to-do people from Pittsburgh, going for a vacation at the lake with their children, servants, and parasols, etc. Roscoe told us that they also arrive on the train. There are drivers in buggies and spring wagons waiting at the depot to take them to the lake.

We drove two miles along a scenic country road. We traveled through the woods alongside South Fork Creek, with the chorus of birdsong ringing from the newly leafed out trees, and wildflowers blooming by the wayside. The horses' hoofs clumped rhythmically on the hard-packed dirt road. They began to pick up speed as we neared our destination, seeming to know that we were almost there. The air was wondrously fresh and fragrant. We drew deep, heady breaths of it.

It tasted like wine after being used to the air at Johnstown. We passed Lamb's Bridge, and went on up the valley.

Soon we could see the tremendous dam! There is no water flowing down over the top of the dam, as I used to think. It's just a big embankment or dyke to hold the mountain lake in. The water all comes down over the seventy-foot wide spillway that has been cut through the solid rock in the hillside against which the dam is anchored, and where no erosion can occur. Roscoe tied the horses to a sapling. We walked out to the wooden bridge, close to where the water comes crashing down over the rocks under the spillway. Iris clung to my hand, but Patrick and Morgan pranced from one side of the bridge to the other, acting as if they'd like nothing better than to dive into the water. Roscoe explained that the big dam is an earth dam. That's why it is so very important that no water flows down over the top of it—it would be highly susceptible to erosion. Another thing that is important is that no internal seepage occurs. He explained that it was built of successive layers of clay and coated with huge rocks (so big that it took three teams of horses to move them), and such a dam, if properly built and maintained, can safely contain tremendous bodies of water. The base of the dam is around two hundred seventy feet thick, but across the top, or the breast of the dam it is only about twenty feet broad. The road travels across the top.

By looking at the dam, you would never imagine it to be manmade; it is covered with bushes, saplings, and mountain laurel, vines and wild grasses pushing up from between the rock. It all just looks like a natural part of the landscape. We stood there watching the water come tumbling down from the spillway, over dark boulders and deep crevices, and crashing into the whirlpool below, awed by its rugged, picturesque beauty.

The sun's rays penetrated through the leafy green canopy above. It created a blending of soft light and shadows, truly a place of wild, natural splendor. We then continued on up the road that climbed up to a clump of trees at the top of the dam beside the spillway. There was another wooden bridge up there, directly over the top of the spillway. We stopped on that shady bridge for a while to admire the scenery, then turned around and headed back to where the road forked to the right, out of the trees and into the sunshine and straight across the breast of the dam. At about the middle of the dam, we stopped to take in the breathtaking view—the sheer drop down over the dam to the valley floor below, where we could see the South Fork Creek, Lamb's Bridge, and the road we had just traveled.

But the most interesting view just then, for us, was the one to the left—the dazzling misty Lake Conemaugh! All four hundred and fifty acres of it— two and one half miles long and a mile wide. The water level was just six feet below the top of the dam and appeared to be very deep. The expanse of lake swept away off into the distance and disappeared behind wooded ridges and coves in the beyond. The sky was a dazzling blue above it, or maybe it just seemed bluer, over that great expanse of lake water. There was a farm, with hayfields and orchards, and neatly framed split rail fences on the eastern shore. Beyond the farm was a grassy knoll that jutted out into the lake. Roscoe called it Sheep's Head Point. On the other side there were giant hemlocks, hickories, black birch, sugar maples, and big oak trees crowding the hillside.

Roscoe took some time here to explain to the boys how the big dam and lake came to be; about the canals and barges, and why extra water was needed for the summertime. Also how it became obsolete just two years later when the Pennsylvania railroad came through, and how the South Fork Hunting and Fishing Club bought it for a summer resort.

Just then we heard the sound of hoof beats and the rattle of spring wagon wheels coming over the spillway bridge. When he drew closer we saw that it was Thomas Layton driving, the one who had gotten us permission to come up to the lake. I recognized him from the time he had driven through Johnstown the Sunday afternoon Julie and I had gotten a ride with Patrick and Morgan. He gave us a friendly, courteous welcome, and told us to follow him out to the main grounds of the summer resort colony, where they have their boats.

I was very impressed by the sixteen cottages built along the lake. At least Mr. Layton called them cottages, but they looked more like mansions to me. Some of them were three stories high, with high ceilings, long windows and big porches from which to enjoy the view of the lake. One of them had a round tower at one end, with tinted glass windows, Queen Anne style. Mr. Layton said it had seventeen rooms! But the clubhouse dwarfed them all, with forty-seven rooms, and enough windows and porches for ten houses. There are also a good many boathouses and stables. Everything seemed fairly quiet, but Mr. Layton described how it is in the summertime when the resort is open—with boating parties on the lake on moonlit nights, and the sound of singing and banjoes across the black water, young women in long white dresses and big summer hats, on the arms of well dressed young men in dark suits and derbies, the long front porch crowded with cigar smoking business men. The cottages are lively with noisy big families, happy children, fortunate to be able to have their vacations at the lovely lake, in the bracing fresh air. There were neat lawns and well-tended flowerbeds with hammocks strung between the trees. They have workers tending the lawns, and waitresses to wait on the tables in the clubhouse when the season opens. We then took a woods path down to the lake, drinking in the clear, sweet air, and enjoying the breezes and birdsong.

Mr. Layton said the club owns fifty rowboats, canoes, and sailboats, and even two little steam yachts to putter across the lake in if you wish. He offered to take us out for a ride, and we all unanimously chose a sailboat. Never in my fondest dreams did I ever imagine myself skimming across a great blue mirror of a lake so big that you could see miles and miles of sky in it, with white sails billowing in the breeze and silhouetted against the green woods. At one place we saw two deer come down to the water's edge for a drink. At that point we were behind a ridge and couldn't see the clubhouses and cottages. It all seemed so naturally untamed and picturesque; a majestic mountain scene of peace, loveliness, and wild beauty and, oh, the clear, sweet, unpolluted air! It was like we were in another world, clean, open, and fresh smelling. I wished I could take it with me down to Johnstown.

After our boat ride we said good-bye to Mr. Layton and headed back to our rented horses and wagon. We drove down to the bottom of the spillway waterfall. We found a scenic spot to have our picnic where we could watch the water come crashing down over the boulders. Apparently it was a favorite spot for picnickers, with a ring of stones laid for a fireplace, and a grassy, level spot for our tablecloth. The boys could talk about nothing but the fishing they intended to do after lunch. Iris wanted to find a place where she could go wading. We found wild strawberries everywhere, but unfortunately, they were not yet ripe.

Chloe's picnic lunch was delicious. It seemed all the more so, after the drive we had through the clear, bracing mountain air. Afterward we all stretched out on blankets for a peaceful snooze before packing everything back into the basket and onto the spring wagon.

We headed back down the road, the way we had come, down to the South Fork Creek near Lamb's Bridge—the boy's chosen fishing spot.

South Fork Creek is one of the best trout streams in the state of Pennsylvania. That's why the boys were so excited. Roscoe tied the horses to a post, and we all headed for the creek bank. Iris kicked off her shoes, but after sticking a toe into the water, she squealed and backed away—it was icy cold! After that she was satisfied to sit on the bank and pick forget-me-nots. The creek was about twenty feet across, shallow and swift, but with a deep pool nearby according to the boys, a perfect place for trout fishing. Roscoe helped them to get started and then came to sit beside me on the big fallen log nearby. He asked how I was enjoying the day. I'm sure he wouldn't have needed to ask. He could see that it was one of the most enjoyable days of my life, and I told him so. By way of replying, he said that we would have to have a family outing like this again next year here at the dam, and every spring after that, too. We? I glanced at him quickly, wondering if he had meant anything by that. But I couldn't tell by the expression on his face. He had his chin cupped in his hand and was gazing at the water rushing over the rocks. The next moment he was turning to me with a smile, and saying, "You do so well with Iris . . . she adores you, and I . . ."

At that moment he was interrupted by a yell from Patrick, saying that he had a tug on his line. The fishing got exciting then. They were pulling in one trout after the other. Iris tried to catch a dragonfly and slipped off the bank and fell into the water with a splash! My, such a fuss! I got her out of her wet clothes and wrapped her in a blanket while Roscoe built a small bonfire to dry her clothes. Our conversation after that was mostly about the lake and dam. So I never found out what he was planning to say and if it had any significance. I've been thinking (and praying) about what my answer would be should he propose . . . I'd feel positively scared, and woefully inadequate! But then I call myself a silly goose and quit thinking along these lines. I try to leave my future in God's hands.

We talked about the yearly spring rumors about the dam breaking, wondering if there really ever was any real danger, or if it's all just the idea of having such a mighty body of water "above" us on the mountain. Roscoe said there are several things that might be a problem some day. One of them is the screen of iron rods they put across the spillway to keep the fish from going down over. If, during a cloudburst or flood, it should become clogged with debris, it could raise the water level of the lake high enough for it to start flowing down over the earth dam. If it should wash a gully there, and start to rush through, then . . . well, we just won't think about it. Maybe they could take away the screen before that could happen. He also said something about there having been discharge pipes and a control tower there at one time. They aren't there anymore, which would make it impossible for them to lower the level of the lake should it be necessary. Oh well, I suppose those men know what they're doing. The Johnstown men who checked it out have pronounced the dam safe. There's no use worrying.

Since I've seen those lovely cottages there by the lake, I've been dreaming of living in one of them; yes, with Roscoe, Iris, the boys and Chloe. Now that would be a dream come true, even though I'd be nothing more than Iris' governess. (Smiles).

June 10

*W*hy don't you laugh? Don't let your spirits wilt.
Don't sit and cry over the milk you've spilt.
If you would mend it now, pray let me tell you how.
Just milk another cow! Why don't you laugh?

Anonymous

I'd laugh if it would do any good, but I'm afraid crying would go better. I'm feeling blue and discouraged tonight because Meredith and I have had a spat.

And I mean a SPAT (in capital letters).

Oh dear, after all those high and holy resolutions to treat her with kindness and remembering "Whatsoever ye do unto the least of these My brethren, ye do it unto Me." I wonder how I'm supposed to milk another cow in this case, as the poem says. I apologized to Meredith, then had a talk with Mama. I told her how discouraged I am about what happened, and about my lack of patience and forbearance. She said that it is not those who fall that are failures, but those who fail to get up after they fall. She added, "The mercies of the Lord are new every morning—confess it to the Lord, trust in His forgiveness, and be of good courage. Discouragement is like a baby—the more you nurse it, the bigger it will grow." I had to laugh at that, but I suppose there's some truth to it. Tonight she handed me a clipping, and asked me to make a copy of it for a reminder that discouragement is not of the Lord. I'll copy it here:

Beware of the Evil Tool

A Chinese legend describes how the father of sin decided to have a sale and dispose of all his tools to anyone who would pay the price.

The implements were laid out in a row for inspection, and among others were tools labeled "Malice," "Envy," "Hatred," "Jealousy," and "Deceit." Every one had a price tag on it. Apart from the others lay a harmless looking, wedge-shaped tool, very much worn from use, which was priced a great deal higher than the rest.

One of the buyers asked the devil what it was. "That," he answered, "is Discouragement, and it's in fine shape."

"But why have you priced it so high?"

"Because it is more useful to me than any of the others. I can pry open and get inside a man's consciousness with that wedge when I couldn't get near him with any of the others. And believe me, once I do get inside I can use that man in whatever way suits me best. Of course, you'll notice it is well worn. That's because I use it with nearly everybody, for very few of you mortals know that it belongs to me."

However, the price was so high that this particular tool was never sold. The devil still owns it and is still using it.

After I had copied this, Mama came back and sat on the rocker by the fireplace. We talked about the sermon we heard at church this forenoon, which was on sanctification. We were told that there are two natures in the believer, and so two ways of seeking holiness. The one is striving for it with our utmost efforts and resolutions, and trusting Christ to help us in doing so, but failing time and time again. The other—the only way to victory—is to abide in Christ and trust Him to work out His sanctification in us. It is not possible to purge the flesh from sinful inclinations and practicing holiness by willing and resolving to do the best that lieth in us. Rather must surrender all to Christ and let Him live and work in us and sanctify us by His own power. It was hard for me to comprehend this, but Mama did her best to help me understand. At least, it gave me hope, and helped to rout out that "most useful tool" mentioned in the article.

June 14

Vincent came to the door this morning with his hat full of strawberries, saying that the berries on Hartzall's Hill are ripe. He would take us girls up to pick some if we were ready. Meredith was still in bed—she hardly ever rises before ten. So Julie and I grabbed our sunbonnets and went. We knew that Meredith would be furious if we went without her, but we didn't care.

In a way it seemed almost like old times. I couldn't help but think of last year—how merry and happy we had been on our annual berry-picking excursion. I remembered the special attention and extra courtesies Vincent had bestowed on Julie and of his sisterly kindness to me. Everything has changed now, and all because of Meredith's coming. But Papa says that God's hand is in everything. We must trust Him to work all things out for good.

Vincent had his span of horses hitched to the spring wagon, and we, with our bowls, clambered on the back. What a beautiful morning it was. How pleasant was the drive up there with the robins so sweetly and joyously singing; everything so fresh and dewy. The air was so fragrant with the scent of wild roses blooming along the fencerow. Someday, I think I'd like to have a little house built up there, away from the fumes and clutter of the city. Vincent was his usual amiable and lovable self. He didn't even ask why Meredith hadn't come. Maybe (hopefully) he was just a little bit fed up with her (shame on me).

When we came back with our bowls filled with berries, and were in the midst of capping them and cooking jams and jellies, she came down the stairs, still looking tousled and sleepy-eyed. When we told her that Vincent had taken us berrying, a spark of jealousy flashed into her eyes. Just as I had thought, it infuriated her. She gallantly fought to gain control. She declined helping with the berries, saying she had slept poorly and felt exhausted, and would I please kindly run upstairs and bring down her parasol? She needed to go down to Paxton's store for a few items. Although I was rebelling inwardly, I did fetch it for her. Her room looked like a tornado had gone through, with clothes strewn about, powder spilt on her bureau, and magazines tossed here and there. I wonder how she can stand being in the midst of such disarray. It makes Pearl grumble, and she has often "given warning." But Pearl always relents and cleans her room, sooner or later.

Julie made a scrumptious strawberry pie for supper. Since Vincent's aunt and uncle are in Ebensburg for a week, we invited him over for the meal. Meredith had forgotten her spite by then, and was as blithe and merry as a lark. Vincent matched her mood. As usual, Julie was quiet and subdued in their presence. I'm sure that none of us has realized the depth of her suffering. She puts up a brave and cheerful front.

The fragrant climbing roses on the porch trellis are in bloom. Mama has brought in a bouquet of them. They fill the library with their hauntingly sweet fragrance. June must be the loveliest month.

June 17

Vincent and Meredith have announced their engagement! They returned this afternoon from a drive to Mineral Point, tied the horses, came in together, and Vincent broke the news. He sure looked happy. Meredith looked very self-satisfied and pleased with herself. I think Julie was a bit stunned because she told me, after they left, that all along she's been entertaining the hope that they would break up before it came to this. They plan to be married in October. We are to have the wedding here at our house. That means some busy months ahead. It will be exciting, though. If it weren't for Julie's sadness (and our dashed hopes of ever having Vincent in the family), it would be downright thrilling and romantic. I doubt if this house has ever seen a wedding in it before. We'll do our best to make it a beautiful one. Meredith complains a lot these days (about the house). She wishes we'd have Brussels carpets, elegant damask draperies, queens ware, fine heirloom furniture. She grumbles about all Papa gives away to the "shiftless poor" who could manage very well themselves if they'd be willing to work. She rarely offers to lift a finger herself to help with the work. She's too much of a "lady." But . . . oops! I'm forgetting my resolution . . .

She came down the stairs tonight, looking absolutely stunning, dressed in her very finest, and her honey-colored hair coiffed to perfection. Her dress was of pale pink with silver sprigs, and had a wide, flaring skirt. Her black evening wrap contrasted well with the pink. Her silver high-heeled shoes added the finishing touch. After she had gone, Pearl snorted out some caustic remarks about how scandalously she had "minced" out the door, putting on condescending airs. Julie and I had to giggle at Pearl's way of describing her to a T. I said, "Oh well, maybe Vincent will tone her down a bit, for he's such a likeable down-to-earth chap." Pearl gave another snort of derision, and shot back, "Tone her down, my eye. It's her that will be dragging him down, the hussy."

Julie and I took a walk out to the orchard tonight, just as twilight was descending. All was peaceful, and the birds were twittering their goodnights. We were thankful that we still had each other. There were so many abundant blessings to be counted. It was such a lovely June evening.

PART THREE
Dreams and Heartaches

*A*nother well-spent day with Dr. & Mrs. Dave. A heavy thunderstorm came up in the afternoon with bright white streaks of lightning, loud crashing thunder, and a heavy downpour. Dr. Dave told us to come into the library; we'd have our tea there, a bit early. There I felt quite safe from the storm while the dear old couple reminisced about by-gone days. Someone had sent them a stack of old Detroit Free Press papers. I spent some time skimming through them. An article entitled "Little Mother" caught my eye. I asked them if I could bring it along home to copy. It was about the heroic actions of a thirteen-year-old girl named Bess, who saved her little brother and sisters from drowning. With all the talks about floods in this area, it's kind of interesting to read something like that. I'll copy it here:

Little Mother

She was a clear-eyed, fresh-cheeked little maiden, living on the banks of the great Mississippi, the oldest of four children, and mother's "little woman" always. They called her so because of her quiet, matronly care of the younger Mayfields—that was her father's name. Her own name was the beautiful one of Elizabeth, but they shortened it to Bess.

She was thirteen when one day Mr. Mayfield and his wife were called to the nearest town, six miles away. "Be mother's little woman, dear," said Mrs. Mayfield, as she kissed the rosy face. Her husband added, "I leave the children in your care, Bess. Be a little mother to them."

Bess waved her old sunbonnet vigorously, and held up the baby Rose, that she might watch them to the last. Old Daddy Jim and Mammy had been detailed by Mr. Mayfield to keep an unsuspected watch on the little nestlings, and were to sleep at the house. Thus, two days went by, when Daddy Jim and Mammy begged to be allowed to go to the quarters where the Negroes lived, to see their daughter "Jinnie" who was pow'ful bad wid the toothache." They declared they would be back by evening, so Bess was willing. She put the little girls to bed, and persuaded Rob to go; then seated herself by the table with her mother's workbasket in quaint imitation of Mrs. Mayfield's industry in the evening time. But what was this? Her feet touched something cold! She bent down and felt around with her hand. A pool of water was spreading over the floor. She knew what it was; the Mississippi had broken through the levee. What should she do? Mammy's stories of how houses had been washed away, and broken in pieces, were in her mind. "Oh, if I had a boat," she exclaimed, "but there isn't anything of the sort on the place." She ran wildly out to look for Mammy; and stumbled over something setting near the edge of the porch. A sudden inspiration took her. Here was her boat: A very large old-fashioned oblong tub. The water was now several inches deep on the porch, and she contrived to half float, half roll the tub into the room.

Without frightening the children she got them dressed in the warmest clothes they had. She lined the oblong tub with a blanket, and made ready bread and cold meat left over from supper. With Rob's assistance, she dragged the tub upstairs. There was a single large window in the room, and they set the tub directly by it, so that when the water rose the tub would float out. There was no way for the children to reach the roof, which was a very steep inclined one. It did not seem long before the water had very nearly risen to the top of the stairs leading from below.

Bess flung the window open and made Rob get into their novel boat. Then she lifted in Kate. Finally baby Rose, who began to cry, was given into Rob's arms, and now the little mother taking the basket of food, made ready to enter, too, but lo! There was no room for her with safety to the rest. Bess paused a moment, drew

*a long breath, and kissed the children quietly.
She explained to Rob that he must guard the
basket, and that they must all sit till. Good-by,
dears. Say a prayer for sister. Rob, if you ever
see father and mother, tell them I took care of
you! Then the water seized the insecure vessel,
and out into the dark night it floated.*

*The next day Mr. Mayfield, who, with his
neighbors scoured the broad lake of eddying
water that represented the Mississippi,
discovered the tub lodged in the branches of a
sycamore with the children weeping and chilled,
but safe. And Bess? Ah, where was Bess, the
"little mother" who in that brief moment resigned
herself to death. They found her later, floating
on the water with her brave childish face turned
to the sky; and as strong arms lifted her into the
boat, the tears from every eye paid worthy
tribute to the "little mother."*

Detroit Free Press

It's a sad story, and reading things like that could
add fuel to fears of the people like Mrs. Bessie Oliver
when there are warnings of flooding in Johnstown.
But Papa says that nowadays people are becoming
calloused to the warnings—they have tired of hearing
about a disaster that never happens. Most people
don't take the warnings to heart. Some of them like
to make jokes about the South Fork dam bursting.

Let's hope it remains nothing but a joke.

The weather has cleared tonight and a sliver of a moon is rising up over the mountain. Julie and I plan to go down to Aunt Rolla's to make taffy. We'll try not to think back to the days when Vincent was always along (and without Meredith, of course) adding spice and life to the party. Roscoe is on a business trip to Pittsburgh. The children's Aunt Winifred is here from Pittsburgh for the weekend. I always miss them all until the next time I'm there again. I do dearly love my job as Iris' governess!

Time to go. Papa is at the gate with the mare hitched to the buggy to drive us down to Uncle Otto's. Good-bye for now.

July 14

I'm still fuming a bit as I write this. I had a date with Roscoe tonight, and when I opened my closet door to get out my best evening dress, I found it lying on the floor, all crumpled on a heap, and soiled besides! I knew in a flash that Meredith must have worn it. Her, with all her fine dresses, and here I have only one good evening dress and she has to wear it. I had seen her come down the stairs this afternoon, all dressed up to go out, and Vincent was waiting at the gate with his buggy. As she flounced out the door, she called back, "Vincent and I are going house hunting." I was busy at the sewing machine with some mending, and never even noticed what she was wearing. I suppose her own dresses are all too good for something as menial as house hunting. So she wore mine. She probably figured it was too common to be an evening dress. Well, there was only one thing left to do—wear one of hers! And so I did, choosing the lavender lawn with the row of ruffles. I felt kind of silly and uncomfortable with it, but Roscoe thought it was lovely. But, woe is me; when I got home at 1 a.m. and tiptoed up the stairs in my stocking feet, Meredith was waiting for me. She stood in the middle of my room with her hands on her hips and her eyes flashing! She was furious. If one can give a tongue lashing without raising one's voice above a whisper I got one. The nerve of her—after wearing my dress. But already I'm cooling off. I know that her dress was much finer than mine. And, in between our spats, we really do get along very well. We're both trying, or rather, all of us are. Julie and the others have their run-ins with her sometimes, too. Just four more months, and then she'll move away. We'll be left with nothing but regrets if we don't do our best to treat her civilly.

Roscoe and I had a grand time—there was a band concert in the park. It was lively. I'm wondering if he will speak out soon. I can't understand myself, finding myself wishing he wouldn't. I wish things would just stay as they are now. Maybe it's because Papa and Mama aren't very enthused about the idea. Strangely, whenever they say something about it, it immediately fills me with a desire to do just what they are reluctant about. I guess I'm not really sure what I want. I'll leave it all in God's hands.

Time to head for bed. I'm yawning. It's very late. Tomorrow there are church services. Goodnight, old journal.

July 15 Sunday

Our sermon today at church was entitled, "Salvation in the Ark of God," using the story of the Flood in Genesis as a parallel illustration—the drowning people outside the ark could have had salvation, had they listened to Noah during their "day of grace." They spurned his warnings until calamity came upon them and it was too late. They cried for him to open the door to the ark, but God had sealed the door. Noah could not open for them. So it is today. If we listen to God's voice, harden not our hearts and come to Him now, entering into the Ark of Salvation—justified by His grace through the redemption that is in Christ Jesus, we need not fear when floods and calamities come.

We invited the Hollis's for supper. It was a special evening for us all. They are such a dear old couple, always gracious, kind and loving. Aunt Rolla and Uncle Otto came up later. We sat on the porch to catch the cooler evening breeze, visiting until the stars came out. The fireflies flickered mysteriously over the garden, and danced among the shadows in the orchard. "I'm glad we don't live right smack down in the middle of Johnstown. Up here, when the moon shines, it seems almost as if we're out in the country."

Mrs. Dave related a rather amusing, yet pathetic experience she once had. Last winter, one snowy day when she was walking down the street, just outside Colbert's store she heard the sound of sobbing, and a little voice praying pleadingly. She stopped, and saw a little boy with his face pressed against the store window, rubbing his eyes with hands that were blue with cold. She asked what he was doing. He said he was praying—asking God to give him a pair of mittens. So Mrs. Dave took him into the store and warmed his hands. She bought him a pair of good warm mittens. He smiled up at her; his eyes filled with awe and gratitude, and wonderingly asked, "Are you God's mother?"

The re-telling of it brought tears to her eyes, and ours as well. There are so many needy people, some hungry and homeless, and all needing to hear the good news of the gospel. I caught myself thinking, maybe someday, when and if I ever am the second Mrs. Eldridge, what a lot I could give to the poor. But then I blushed with shame at my presumptuousness, glad that no one could read my thoughts. I just heard the sound of hoof beats through the open window in my room, which must be Vincent bringing Meredith home. From down in Johnstown the sounds of singing and happy children playing come floating up on the evening breeze. My thoughts travel to the big

Lake Conemaugh, where there are probably boating parties going on right now. The sounds of music and banjo playing are borne across the lake to the ladies and gentlemen on the clubhouse porch.

Today was a perfect day for sailing, and I, in my mind's eye, could see the white sails billowing and the boats skimming across the mirror-like lake. Maybe if I'd throw a few hints to Roscoe, we could have another outing up there this summer. But perhaps the place is too full of the rich Pittsburgh people in the summertime. Oh well, it doesn't hurt to dream, as long as I tell no one but my journal. (Smiles).

July 18

Vincent and Meredith have found themselves a house down on Washington Street. It's sturdily built, but far from new. It is a pine board bungalow with vines growing way up over the porch roof, and a tiny kitchen garden plot beside it. Vincent is really enthused about it, and says it will be "right nice" after the necessary repairs are made, and it's fixed up and decorated. He doesn't seem to notice that Meredith appears to not entirely share his enthusiasm. They came in the afternoon to tell us about it. She seemed rather quiet. After Vincent had left we pressed her for more details. She wrinkled her nose and said it's rather dingy. The street is noisy, but she would try to be satisfied since it's the best Vincent can do for now.

Julie said afterward that she could have shaken her. I knew what she meant because I know she'd be more than willing to live in even a hovel with Vincent. She still cares deeply and can't bear to see Meredith shrug off what Vincent is doing for her as if it were nothing.

Vincent came again tonight to plan the fixing of the house, and its furnishings. He seemed to be supremely happy, all kindness and thoughtfulness. But I think his joy was dampened somewhat when he couldn't seem to please Meredith in their plans. She wanted this and she wanted that. His face would cloud over as he explained—it would be lovely, but he would be too heavily in debt if they got it now. He added, "Sometime we'll have it your way, but for now we must cut the garment according to the cloth." Meredith pouted a bit, but gave in at last. She became pliable and sweet, although Julie and I thought it seemed a little forced and artificial. But by the time Vincent was ready to leave she was bright-faced and starry-eyed again. It reminded me of what Pearl once said about Meredith: "She can pretend to be as shy and demure as a nun— but watch those claws—she can scratch like a cat." I laughed merrily when she said it. Now it doesn't seem so funny anymore when it's our Vincent she might scratch. Before they went out the door, I overheard Vincent saying, laughingly, that he would be working like an ox to get the nest ready for the bird. And Meredith's tinkling, put-on laugh floated back to us.

When she came back in, her face looked more like a storm cloud than the starry-eyed happiness of a soon-to-be married gal getting her nest ready, as Pearl said later.

"It's not fair," she complained bitterly. "After all my dreams of living in a . . . a . . . dream house," she finished, after a pause. Pearl was looking daggers at her, most likely thinking things not lawful to be uttered. Julie, not being able to bear hearing more, slipped off into the library.

"I always wanted a Steinway piano," Meredith was going on with her tirade. "And I can't see why we can't have one. I want mosquette carpets, if we can't have Brussels. They tread so softly. If they'd be an extravagance, they'd be worth it."

I, too, found I couldn't bear to hear more and came up to my room to pour it all out in my journal, wondering for the forty-thousandth time why Meredith ever had to come and live here.

Now I'm sitting here on the window seat, watching a pair of squirrels scampering around on the branches of the big oak tree. They're so agile and lively, and I think I'll try to sketch them.

July 20

Today at the Eldridge's, Iris was all excited about a box full of ducklings a neighbor gave her. She put them into the fountain to splash around in, laughing in delightful glee when they swam under the splashing sprinklers. Roscoe had just gotten a work crew in to rake, prune, trim and weed the lawn and garden. Old Boas, the gardener, can't keep up. He wants everything to be ship-shape, and it is, too. As I surveyed the entire outdoors elegance—the land-scaping, the huge columns on the front porch, the statues and the fountain, and thought of the elegance of the house and all the luxuries inside, my heart felt a little sore. Would I be happy as the mistress of such grand opulence? I know that deep down, my heart shies away from it, and yet Roscoe is so nice, and the boys, and especially little Iris. Even old Chloe is becoming very dear to me. The other day I found her at the table, surrounded by her pots and pans, with her head down on her arms, fast asleep. She awoke with a start as I entered, and blinking her eyes, said apologetically, "I was dat tired in m'bones dat I don drapped off to sleep arsidentally." What would we do without her 'rasslin in pra'r' for us all?

Now, if I were Meredith . . . or like her . . . how I would revel in and love all the luxuries and grandness and riches Roscoe has to offer. The rich, plush carpets, the elegant lace curtains, the grand Steinway piano and other furnishings, etc. I had a most hilar-ious thought . . . what would she say if I'd suggest her that we trade . . . she could have Roscoe with his riches, and I could have Vincent. I'd trade any day. I'm almost sure Meredith would, too, but I don't know about the men—or rather, I *do* know. I'd still have to adopt Iris in the bargain. Time to stop thinking such silly nonsense and get to bed. I have a vacation coming up next week—all next week. Roscoe is taking his family to visit their maternal grandmother for a week. I haven't decided yet what I want to do with my time. Maybe just relax, for a change. Goodnight.

July 23

We're having a heat wave just now. Shimmering heat lightning is flashing over the Allegheny Mountains nearly every evening. Vincent is head-over-heels into the renovations at his "new" house. He was here last evening. When I offered to help him in the house on my week off, he accepted so gratefully that Julie shored up her courage and offered to help, too. You see, we pitied him. When he had asked Meredith if she wanted to help, she declined politely, saying he would have to hire help; she wasn't made for that kind of thing. Besides, she was packing her bags for a week's vacation at Lake Conemaugh (lucky thing!). A well-to-do friend of hers has invited her to join her there as her guest for a week. I couldn't help but feel a twinge of jealousy (or maybe I should say more than just a twinge.) How does she get all the lucky breaks? Before she left, Vincent asked for her opinion on several things he's doing in the house, but to everything she merely replied, "Do what you think is best, it doesn't matter much to me." I could have shaken her for her "couldn't care less" attitude. She sure doesn't seem to have much of an interest in the house, the spoiled thing. (Ooops! Excuse me!) Anyway, that was when Julie and I offered to help. I couldn't help but think of how much fun this would all be if it were Julie we were getting the house ready for, and she was to be the bride. (Sigh).

But we'll still have fun, for Vincent seems to be in high spirits. Maybe he knows Meredith better than we do. We just haven't seen all her good points yet, or learned how to appreciate them.

Tonight I went for a short walk up the hillside, hoping it would be cooler there under the shady, leafy trees. It wasn't cooler; there was no breeze. It was still refreshing and peaceful. I watched a tiny striped chipmunk playing near a fallen log, darting here and there, and watching me with bright, inquisitive eyes. I love to go up there when the wind sighs through the pines, making a melody all its own. Tonight they were silent, like tall sentinels on the mountain: So far away, and yet so near to the hustle and bustle of Johnstown below.

July 24

Julie and I spent the day at Vincent's bungalow, with kerchiefs tied over our heads and wearing our oldest clothes. Vincent was hammering and sawing, making new cellar steps. We were painting the woodwork in the kitchen. He kept us both feeling jolly and at ease—with his gay repartee and good-hearted congeniality. It really was a lot of fun putting in a day's work alongside of Julie once again. She's a good sport, and doesn't seem to have a jealous bone in her body.

The house is rather a cute little cottage. We still feel really indignant with Meredith for being so indifferent. What a cozy love nest it would make!

It seemed so much like old times. We enjoyed being with Vincent so much again, that I was horrified to catch myself thinking of what a lot of problems it would solve if the sailboat Meredith is probably sailing on this very minute should sink to the bottom of the lake! I cast the thought aside immediately, repented of my uncharitableness, and asked God to forgive me. Shame on me!

When it was time to head home to clean up for supper, we had gotten a lot accomplished and it was a very satisfying feeling. Tired, but happy, we, at Vincent's call of "all aboard!" climbed on the back of his spring wagon. Cavalier trotted briskly homeward. Passing Uncle Otto's house, Aunt Rolla stood on the porch, waving a tea towel, looking as if she had important news to tell. Vincent reined the horse to a stop. She came out to the wagon. "Did you hear there's a scarlet fever scare here in Johnstown?" she asked. "There are at least a dozen children who have it. It is expected to spread fast."

Oh no! I'm glad that the Eldridges are safely away in Pittsburgh—perhaps we should send word to them to stay until the scare is over. Scarlet fever in the midst of a heat wave! Oh dear, what next?

*A*pall of gloom hangs over Johnstown, with the spread of the scarlet fever. Roscoe sent word from Pittsburgh on Friday that Iris came down with it the day after they arrived in Pittsburgh. They will stay until she's well again. They've hired a private nurse for her. There was not a word of how she's doing or how bad it really is. I went over to see Chloe who is at home alone in the big mansion with the other servants. She was practically beside herself, 'rasslin in pra'r. Unashamedly, I joined her in interceding for the "pore honey lamb chile." She stayed on her knees so long that she 'cotched' another misery in her back. But she was victorious, for after awhile she got up with a "light of glory" on her kindly old black face, and a big smile, saying that "de Lord had done tole her a dat wee honey lamb" was getting better. I went home in better spirits than I had gone, needless to say.

Meredith came home from Lake Conemaugh sooner than she had planned. Everyone had been evacuated—sent home because of the scarlet fever scare. She was 'out of sorts' about it. She had been cheated out of her full vacation. She didn't seem to have a twinge of mercy for the suffering ones.

*O*n Saturday at the Hollis's I read a piece in an old magazine entitled "Kiss Me, Mama." That brought tears to my eyes. I am wondering how little Iris is, with no Mama there to kiss her. I'll copy it here:

Kiss Me, Mama

The child was so sensitive, so like that little shrinking plant that curls at the breath, and shuts its heart from the light. The only beauties she possessed were an exceedingly transparent skin, and the most mournful large blue eyes.

A very stern, strict, conscientious mother had trained me, but I was a hardy plant, rebounding after every shock; misfortune could not daunt, though discipline tamed me. I fancied, alas! I must go through the same routing with this delicate creature; so one day, when she had displeased me exceedingly by repeating an offense, I was determined to punish her severely. I was very serious all day, and upon sending her to her little couch I said: "Now, my daughter, to punish you, and show you how very, very naughty you have been, I shall not kiss you tonight."

She stood looking at me, astonishment personified, with her great mournful eyes wide open—I suppose she had forgotten her misconduct until then; and I left her with big tears dropping down her cheeks, and her little red lips quivering.

Presently I was sent for. "Oh, Mama! You will kiss me; I can't go to sleep if you don't!" she sobbed, every tone of her voice trembling. She held out her little hands.

Now came the struggle between love and what I falsely termed duty. My heart said, "Give her a kiss of peace." My stern nature urged me to persist in my correction, that I might impress the fault upon her mind. This was the way I had been trained, till I was a most submissive child; and I remembered how I had often thanked my mother since for her straightforward course.

I knelt by the bedside. "Mother can't kiss you, Ellen," I whispered, though every word choked me. Her hand touched mine, it was very hot, but I attributed it to her excitement. She turned her little grieving face to the wall; I blamed myself as the fragile form shook with suppressed sobs, and saying: "Mother hopes little Ellen will learn to mind after this," left the room for the night. Alas! In my desire to be severe I forgot to be forgiving.

It must have been twelve o'clock when my nurse awakened me. Apprehensive, I ran eagerly to the child's chamber; I had had a fearful dream.

Ellen didn't know me. She was sitting up, crimsoned from the forehead to the throat, her eyes so bright that I almost drew back aghast at their glances.

From that night a raging fever drank up her life; and what was the incessant thought poured into my anguished heart? "Oh! Kiss me mama, do kiss me; I can't go to sleep. I won't be naughty if you'll only kiss me! Oh, kiss me, dear Mama; I can't go to sleep."

Little angel! She did go to sleep one gray morning, and she never woke again, never! Her hand was locked in mine, and all my veins grew icy with its gradual chill. Faintly the light faded out of the beautiful eyes, whiter and whiter grew the tremulous lips. She never knew me, but with her last breath she whispered, "I will be good, Mama, if you'll only kiss me."

Kiss her! God knows how passionately but unavailing were my kisses upon her cheek and lips after that fatal night. God knows how wild were my prayers that she might know, if but only once, that I kissed her. God knows how I would have given up my very life could I have asked forgiveness of that sweet child.

*Grief is unavailing now! She lies in her little
tomb. There is a marble urn at the head, and a
rosebush at her feet; there grow sweet summer
flowers; there waves the grass; there birds sing
there matins and their vespers; there the blue
sky smiles down to day and there lies buried
the freshness of my heart.*

Selected.

I don't believe there's anyone alive who can read
that through with dry eyes. It makes me long to go to
Iris, and have her throw her arms around me, and be
able to make her feel better. I have to wonder, is she
calling for me, or perhaps for her lost mother? I know
she has the best of care. Roscoe is there for her, and
yet, to a child, no arms can comfort like a mother's
arms.

August 13

The Eldridges are back, and little Iris is well on
the road to recovery. Chloe is "singing de
praises" all day long—folk songs and gospel tunes. I
join in on the ones I know. The whole family is happy
about it, of course. Tonight when Roscoe brought me
home in the buggy he told me all the details of her
illness. And yes, she did call for me, even in her
delirium. There was a tender expression on Roscoe's
face as he talked about his little motherless daughter.

His eyes were bright with unshed tears, some of them probably tears of gratitude.

We had just rounded a street corner when we heard yells from bystanders, and a loud "Whoa! Whoa!" from the direction of a wildly careening oncoming carriage with two horses hitched. The runaway horses were galloping wildly. Men seemed to spring out of nowhere trying to catch them. The horses swerved and ran up over the curb unto the sidewalk. We heard a woman scream. The carriage missed us by just a few feet, tilting precariously. The horses plunged on. I had watched horrified as the woman on the sidewalk was knocked down. Mindless of my lame leg, I sprang out of the buggy to help her. But when I reached her, she was already up, trembling and brushing off her skirts.

"Meredith!" I gasped. "Have you been hurt?" She shook her head no, yet blinking back the tears. Roscoe had tied the horse to a lamppost and came running, expecting her to be hurt.

"I'm all right," Meredith said, a bit shakily, and looking very woebegone. "It could've been much worse." She was rubbing her elbow. She suddenly burst into tears.

"I'll take you home," Roscoe quickly offered, "if you'll tell me where you live." It dawned on me that Meredith and Roscoe had not met before. I quickly introduced them to each other, and offered to walk the rest of the way home so we would have room for Meredith. By the time I got home, even though I made use of some short cuts through alleys, they were already sitting in the library, apparently having gotten well acquainted in that short time. They were talking away at a great rate. Meredith had recovered her poise, and was looking as impeccable as ever. Roscoe left soon after. Meredith pounced on me—asking all sorts of questions about the Eldridges. She wanted to know if we were engaged, or planning to be soon, and that sort of thing. I evaded her questions as best as I could, and retreated to my room as quickly as I dared, feeling irked and out-of-sorts at their getting acquainted, and her excessive interest.

"Now, that's a fine kettle of fish!" I fumed to Julie later. With her love of riches and ease, she would be apt to throw Vincent over for Roscoe, if she could get him. I was getting angrier by the minute. I hardly knew why, except that I had premonitions of something unpleasant about to happen. I threw myself face down on the bed and had a good cry, after which I felt better. After all, God is in control of these things. It's no use fretting and stewing. As I went down the stairs, I heard Pearl singing heartily:

Courage, brother! Do not stumble
Tho' thy path be dark as night;
There's a star to guide the humble—
Trust in God and do the right.
Let the road be dark and dreary,
And its end far out of sight,

Face it bravely! Strong or weary—
Trust in God and do the right.
—Norman Macleod

Vincent came in tonight and offered to pay Julie and me for the week's work we put in at his house. We declined; telling him it's all a part of our wedding gift to him. I asked him how Meredith had liked it, and couldn't help but notice how his face clouded over.

His answer was, "She didn't say much." That made me more provoked with Meredith than ever. We had worked so hard—painting, sanding, varnishing, stenciling, and then cleaning every room of the house. Vincent had been so happy with the way it looked. She could have at least pretended to be pleased. Grrr!

Enough said about it, dear journal. Let's talk about the weather. It's such a chilly evening that it feels like fall is approaching—very unusual for August. Pearl even tiptoed in and kindled a little fire in my fireplace—she knew I might tell her it isn't necessary. But it does feel good and brightens up the room.

I hear the quavering notes of a screech owl from the tall pine behind the barn, and that, too, reminds me of chilly fall evenings. But summer's not over yet, we'll have over a month more of it, and probably still some uncomfortably sticky weather to be endured.

The yawns and nods are taking over, and so I'll say goodnight.

*T*he scarlet fever scare is receding, thanks to the modern medicines they have nowadays—praise God!

But now there's another trouble. Things don't seem to be going the best between Vincent and Meredith. Julie and I are beginning to wonder whether the plans for having a wedding here at our house are beginning to fall through. It's a rather alarming thought. There really must be something wrong. On Saturday night he brought her home early. Meredith stormed into the house, her face looking like a thundercloud. She slammed the door and ran up the steps to her room.

Uncle Otto and Aunt Rolla were just coming up the drive as Vincent started down. They said his face was white and set and he didn't even notice their friendly wave, or else he chose not to return it. He hasn't been back since. Papa and Uncle Otto have already re-papered both the library and drawing room with fresh wallpaper in preparation for the wedding. Mama and Pearl with Julie's help have also done a lot of extra canning. All in all, it would be quite a letdown.

Poor Vincent! What a disappointment for him after getting his house all ready. But perhaps I'm jumping to conclusions after all. I'm sure they've had spats before, though none that lasted this long. Surely Meredith will come to her senses after awhile and go back and ask forgiveness. She'll put on her pretty charms again, and everything will be all right. It all gives me a queer feeling inside.

*V*incent did come back on Saturday night in the buggy with Cavalier. Meredith was all dressed up and waiting for him. It would've been interesting to be a little mouse under the buggy seat, to hear what was being said. Apparently things are better now between them, but not like before. They didn't stay long. Vincent didn't come in when they returned.

When she came in, Meredith, in a detached tone of voice, announced that the wedding was to be postponed until spring. Julie and I were shocked, but both Mama and Papa looked a bit relieved. Pearl positively crowed. I just don't have much heart for journal writing, so goodnight for now.

*F*or a long time Mama has had the notion to invite the Eldridge family over for Sunday dinner. Finally, on Sunday it happened. I wasn't really overly enthused about inviting them into our humble home, when they're used to such finery and elegance. Mama didn't seem to think it would matter. Uncle Otto and Aunt Rolla were invited, too. Vincent was invited also, but he had a toothache and had to miss out on it. We roasted a stuffed goose with all the fixings. Pearl made her specialty—pecan pie with whipped cream. They all seemed to enjoy it. There was just one thing that marred the day for me—Meredith's shameless coquettish flirtations with Roscoe. It was just like that first evening she was here and Vincent came to supper. Julie was positively scandalized. It's worse now because she's engaged to another man. Roscoe knows she's engaged, but seemed to enjoy her attentions nevertheless.

I've been feeling too disillusioned to even write in my journal these past few days. Mama has been very comforting. I told her that it was a sorry day when Meredith came into our lives. But she claims our part is to forgive and to keep trusting in God's leading. Sometimes He moves in mysterious ways His wonders to perform. If it hadn't been for Meredith's actions, the afternoon would've been really enjoyable—the boys enjoyed a game of horseshoes with Papa and Roscoe. We girls sat on blankets on the grass to watch. Iris curled up happily on my lap. If it hadn't been for Meredith's cheering for Roscoe at his every throw— well, I just won't say more. Goodnight, old journal.

October 19

$\mathcal{T}$he frost is on the pumpkin; the fodders on the shock, and the sorghums have turned blood red against the green of the pines on the mountain. Autumn is usually my favorite time of year. But this year none of us are very happy. Meredith has now broken her engagement to Vincent entirely. It just about breaks our hearts to see how dejected he is. His face set in a mask, always unsmiling. I guess she has scratched him, as Pearl predicted; scratched him right off her list, or out of her book. Our friendly, fun loving, handsomely animated, loveable Vincent, walking around looking like he was at a wake! I told Roscoe the whole story tonight when he was driving me home. He looked quite troubled about it, too. He's leaving for a few days of hunting up in the mountains. He owns a cabin up there. He goes for the big game—deer, bears, and wildcats.

I'm feeling rather forlorn tonight, even though there's a bright, cheery fire crackling merrily on the hearth. So, I guess I'll go hunt up Julie's company. There's a big bank of dark clouds rising rapidly in the west, threatening rain. It's growing chillier, too. Maybe I'll feel more like writing later.

November 2

The sky has a glow of red sunset tonight as I headed down the hill for a stroll, not going anywhere in particular, when I heard the sound of swift hoof beats from behind. It was Vincent, in the buggy, driving Cavalier. He came to a stop beside me, and asked, "Want a ride?" I felt undecided for a few moments. He's not the same Vincent he was—his face is pale and drawn, and he's lost weight. But something in his eyes made me decide to go. I climbed in. He didn't speak until we had gone at least a half-mile, and then he blurted out, "Oh, what a fool I've been!" I desperately wanted to say something to make him feel better, but couldn't think of a thing. So I just asked him, "How have you been?"

He shook his head, and without answering me, said, "I'd like nothing better than to get away—move far away from Johnstown, away from the whispers and stares of curious eyes. But I can't; Uncle is an invalid and needs me. The evenings are the worst," he went on. "I usually hitch Cavalier and go for a long drive—anything to keep me from remembering."

The wind was in our faces. The houses flashed by as the horse picked up speed. Faster and faster went Cavalier, his hooves skimming over the road, his mane and tail flying in the wind. I thought he was running away, and I glanced at Vincent in alarm. Seeing my frightened look, he at last reined in the horse, and said apologetically, "There's no sense in trying to drive away from your troubles."

How I longed to comfort him, knowing his heart must be aching fiercely for his lost happiness. There didn't seem to be anything I could say. At the end of the next street he turned the horse around, and we headed for the river. The sunset was more colorful than ever by then, and I absentmindedly remarked,

"Red at night is a sailor's delight." He made no reply and I wished I hadn't spoken. The wind was rippling over the water. A few loudly quacking ducks rose up with their flapping wings making whistling sounds, and flew off into the night. Vincent drew the horse to a stop, laid the lines on the dash, and leaned back.

"I can't bear to go back to the house just yet," he said dejectedly. "It practically suffocates me. Thanks so much for coming with me tonight—you can't believe how much it means to me. Talk to me, about anything you wish, as long as you keep talking."

My heart ached for his pain. So I did what he asked—chatted away brightly about whatever came to mind—about Chloe and her amusing antics, Iris and her childish charms, Patrick and Morgan, and their latest escapades with the pony, Aunt Rolla and Uncle Otto, and how he seems to enjoy being hen-pecked.

Vincent had to chuckle a bit about that, but it was a rather dry, and humorless chuckle. I longed to tell him that Meredith wasn't worth grieving over. Before long he will thank his lucky stars that she broke the engagement. The moon was high over the mountains when he at last picked up the reins and we headed for home. At our doorstep he asked, "Care to go for another ride tomorrow night?" And, of course, I said yes.

When I came into the library there was Meredith, relating an amusing story, and laughing gaily. I went through to my room without speaking to her; afraid I'd say something I'd be sorry for later. Perhaps she thinks it's an amusing, trifling thing to break a man's heart.

*M*y, the wind feels nippy tonight. There's the feel of a snowstorm on the way. I felt chilled to the bone when I came back from my drive with Vincent. I'm huddled under a quilt in front of the fire. I just re-read my last journal entry of a month ago— of our first drive together on that sad November evening. That was the first of many. We've gone driving almost every evening since. Vincent seems to be more like his old self now—I think he's forgetting the pain that Meredith caused him. He needed me then. Now it's me that needs him. I have a heartache of my own these last few weeks. Meredith is "playing up" to Roscoe now with her seductive charms, her bewitching beauty and outrageous flirtations. He's been taking her to the Washington Street Opera house and who knows where all. I know my feeling of loss isn't as great as Vincent's. I wasn't engaged to Roscoe, and I wasn't sure if it would be God's will if he asked me. It still hurts. And little Iris—it almost makes me wish she had died of the scarlet fever, rather than thinking of her having Meredith for a stepmother. I can't even promise her I'll be a "big sister" anymore.

And Julie—Julie is hurting worse than ever. It must seem to her that now I'm betraying her. She doesn't say anything, but the pain and hurt in her eyes says it all. First Meredith took Vincent away from her. Now she probably thinks that I am just as bad. I long to tell her that it's nothing of the sort. Vincent and I confide in each other like a brother and sister; there's nothing more to it than that. Oh, why can't she see it? Vincent certainly couldn't go running back to her the minute Meredith dropped him—that will come later. But for now he needed someone to help heal his broken heart, and that someone was I. But I know it wouldn't do any good to try and explain it to her. If my own heart hadn't been feeling so bereft of late, I'd have quit going on drives with him, for her sake.

Oh my, what a tangled affair this all seems to be! Mama and Papa seem very concerned. I know they are praying for their daughters.

Vincent told me tonight that he realizes now that he never really was in love with Meredith; he was in love with love. He knows now how shallow and fickle she is. Sometimes I wish I could tell Roscoe, but that would certainly never do at all. Never! I think I'll indulge myself in a good cry tonight.

December 25 Christmas Day

We had a white Christmas, perfect weather for sleighing. Papa read the Christmas story. We exchanged gifts and had our roast turkey dinner— and a delicious one it was, too! Mashed potatoes, bread filling, gravy with giblets, creamed corn, and pumpkin pie with whipped cream. We made enough for a poor family down on Main Street. Vincent, Julie and I took it down on the sleigh. We had a jolly time. Vincent seems like his old self again, almost like a part of the family once more, just as he used to be before Meredith came. Meredith was invited to the Eldridges for the day (and I admit that I still feel a stab of pain about that). It made our day happier with her gone.

This afternoon Vincent hitched his two horses to the sleigh and took Julie and me for a ride to Ebensburg and back. We loved it—huddled under the robes—the exhilarating feel of the wind on our faces, the sleigh bells merrily ringing, and skimming over the gleaming snow. On the way back the sun was already low on the horizon. The calm blue winter twilight over the snow made a lovely picture. I thought back to a year ago when we had done the same thing on Christmas day before Meredith came. I thought of all the troubles she brought with her. Oh well, we learned a lot, and are all a little wiser, except perhaps Roscoe. I remember him and the children in my prayers every day. I trust that all things will work out for good for them, too.

We were hungry again when we got back. So we popped some popcorn, and brought a bowlful of apples up from the cellar. We sat around the fire in the library and had a merry gabfest. Uncle Otto and Aunt Rolla joined us for a late supper. We spent the remainder of the evening singing Christmas carols. It was a wonderful day, precious memories in the making.

*A*nother New Year's Day—a time to make a fresh beginning—forgetting those things which are behind and pressing toward the prize of the high calling of God in Christ Jesus. On Saturday at the Hollis's, Dr. Dave was reminiscing about the war, about the boys in gray and the boys in blue, the thunder of artillery shaking the hills, the battle at Gettysburg where the air was black with shot and shell. He said that thousands of homes were made desolate by the war, but in the end the slaves were freed. We got talking about slavery. Being in a story telling mood, Dr. Dave launched into one tale after another, and oft times made spiritual comparisons afterward. He told of a powerfully built, strong looking black man in chains being put on the auction block to be sold. He stoutly declared that he would not work, and no one would be able to make him. A slave owner, used to this sort of thing, bought him, took him home, and threw him into a deep pit. A stream of water was directed into the pit. The black man was told to operate the pump that would pump the water out of the pit. But the man wouldn't budge; that is—not until the water was so deep that he was in danger of drowning. Then he pumped—forced to work after all!

Dr. Dave had another illustration—also about another slave on the auction block that declared he would not work. The man who bought him took him home on his wagon, talking kindly to him all the while. When they arrived at the plantation, he released him from his chains and kindly gave him his freedom papers. He told the slave he was no longer bound to work for him. The slave was so overcome by such generosity he said he would stay to work for him of his own free will. Dr. Dave went on to say that this is how we ought to serve the Lord—out of love for what He has done for us, not as a slave, but of our own free will. We do not do good works thinking we can earn our salvation by them, but we do them out of gratitude because He has loved and redeemed us. Over our steaming cups of tea and Mrs. Dave's butterscotch tarts, we talked until twilight descended. It was so heartwarming, I wished I could stay and listen longer yet! They're such a delightful old couple, devoted to each other and dear to the hearts of many. If one of them should be taken away, I have to wonder how the other one could go on. Maybe they'll go together when their time comes.

February 28

ear journal, I've been sadly neglecting you of late—almost two months since my last entry. February's almost over. Mama will have to do without a birthday again this year. This month will go down in history as the month of the big tornado, which touched down in Pittsburgh, killing seventeen people. It also blew off a church roof in Loretto, a mountain town twenty miles to the northeast.

I'm still enjoying my job at the Eldridge's, even though Meredith is now a part of the picture (or rather, she intends to be before too long, I think). She is just the kind that would marry for money.

Little Iris is dearer to me than ever, and the boys seem almost like brothers. Oh, oh, I've got to go— Vincent's coming up the drive. He's taking Julie and me to a taffy party in Sang Hollow tonight. He's a bit early. Good-bye for now.

March 20

*M*eredith and Roscoe have announced their engagement. We aren't the least bit surprised, even though it's so soon after she broke her previous engagement. They plan to be married in June.

I think I've given myself up to it, although I can't say it doesn't cause me any heartache at all anymore. There are too many reminders. They crop up in unexpected places. I won't cry about it anymore, unless it would be for Iris. I'll probably lose my job after the wedding. I have to wonder how she'll fare then. Oh well, she'll still have Mammy Chloe as she calls her to look after her. Speaking of Chloe, she is not in a mood that could be described as angelic—when she heard the news about the engagement, her face looked like a thundercloud. She banged her pots and pans around as if she were in a temper. I guess she's seen enough of Meredith to know she won't like her for a mistress. Now why couldn't Roscoe have seen that? The truth is Roscoe has never seen her disagreeable side—no siree—she wouldn't want to jeopardize her chance to marry into money. Well, if I know Chloe, she'll be 'rasslin' in pra'r' for the family, and for the grace to do right by them. Dear old Chloe.

I'm glad the winter's over. We are at last on the threshold of spring. It was a long winter. Things still aren't right between Julie and me. I know she thinks I'm taking Vincent away from her. I can't seem to tell her that isn't the case at all—it's just too soon for him to go back to her. He feels like he played the fool, and has to earn her favor and respect all over again. At least, that's my theory. I have no way to prove he will ever return to her. He's equally nice to both of us. There are signs . . . apparently Julie can't see them, but I can.

I think I'll go for a walk tonight. There's a robin sweetly singing. The weather has turned warm and balmy. The snow melted fast these past few days. It's all running down into the rivers, causing them to rise. Our flood season is coming up, with the usual inconveniences, and anxiety. But living close to the rivers is worth it, to my way of thinking.

April 27

I see that in my last entry I had written about the coming of spring, the mild weather and the robins singing. Well, that sure wasn't the last we saw of Old Man Winter. In April we had the heaviest snow of the whole year—fourteen inches of it! Iris and the boys sure had a lot of fun building a snow fort. The snow was wet, heavy stuff; just right for packing. They made it on the north side of the house, where it doesn't get much sunshine. After it was finished, they poured water over it. It froze solid like a real igloo. It's still there, although it's starting to disintegrate. They're wishing it would stay until May.

May 22

*P*apa says the town fathers gathered today at the City Counsel chambers, to settle various matters of the moment, mainly to amend Section twelve of the Codified Ordinance of the Borough of Johnstown. The word "cow" was inserted after "goat," and now it reads: Any person who shall willfully suffer his horse, mare, gelding, mule, hog, goat, cow, or geese to run at large within the Borough shall for each offense forfeit and pay for each of said animal so running at large, the sum of one dollar . . .

That must've come about because of Mrs. Bessie Oliver's cow running at large through town a while ago. How she got out of her stable no one knows, but she gave a group of boys a merry chase—all the way up to Prospect Hill and back, sparing no one's lawn or garden. I'll bet people will fix their stables and fences securely after this.

There was a notice in the Johnstown Tribune that there is to be a Memorial Day Parade next week. I know from previous years' parades, that it will be a time of gaiety, with flags, banners and flowers everywhere. The streets will be crowded with spectators. It's been nearly thirty years since the war—when Lincoln was calling for volunteers. Of course, I wasn't born yet, but Papa and Mama remember plenty. I hope our nation will never again have to go through something like that.

PART FOUR
The Flood

There's a chilly rainstorm moving in from the west, with sharp, gusty winds blowing down from the mountains. The rain started coming down at four o'clock. At first it was only a fine gentle mist, and later tapered off altogether. At about nine a gentle rain began again. I decided that it's a good night for reading. I snuggled under the quilts with another one of Louisa May Alcott's books, *Under the Lilacs*. I got so absorbed in the book that I forgot the time. I must have dozed off. I was awakened some time later by the sound of heavy rain against the windowpanes—simply pouring down! It's still raining hard. We've surely been having our share of rains lately. My thoughts travel up to the big Lake Conemaugh, imagining what it would be like up there with all that rain pouring down. In three weeks the summer resort will open again for the season. The lucky vacationers will arrive. It's kind of hard to give up my dreams of going back to the lake again in June with the Eldridge family as we had planned last year. Now it will be Meredith, but the children won't be along. The newlyweds plan to spend their honeymoon in one of the cottages. Chloe and I, along with the other "servants," will have the care of the children and house for the two weeks they're away. I'm not sure what the plans are for me after that—whether or not I'm to stay on as governess to Iris. I rather hope so.

Time to get some shut-eye. It's late. Tomorrow morning will roll around all too soon. It sure sounds cozy with the rain coming down in torrents against the windowpanes. Goodnight.

*V*incent stopped in early this morning, saying he's planning to go up to the South Fork Dam at Lake Conemaugh. He's a friend of Thomas Layton's too. They had hard rains up there. He's going to see if he can be of any help. If the dam should spring a leak anywhere, or the iron grill at the spillway become clogged, they might need help before the day is over, especially if the rains continue. He donned his raincoat, saddled up Cavalier, and rode off through the thick mist that hung close to the ground like brushwood. The sky still looked dark and lowering, threatening more rain.

Papa came back from Paxton's store a short time later, saying that he's believes Johnstown is in for a bad time. At five o'clock this morning there was a landslide that caved in the stable at Kress' brewery. The rivers are roaring, and rising a little more than a foot an hour. Julie and I put on our boots and sloshed down to see them. It was an awesome sight. The water was a mighty torrent—muddy and rushing, carrying bobbing logs and driftwood, tearing onward unrelentingly. When the seven o'clock shift arrived at the Cambria Mills, the men were told to go back home to take care of their families. There was water in most of the cellars downtown. Schools were dismissed for the day. The children must have thought it a grand adventure because many were playing in the streets, shouting and splashing in high glee. Those who owned cows were driving them to the hillside, intending to bring them back as soon as the water receded. We overheard one man remark to another that he never before saw a cow drink Stony Creek water on Main Street.

When the rain started to come down again in torrents, Julie and I headed for Aunt Rolla's, knowing full well that we would be scolded as well as pampered there. The wind was rising, and driving the rain against the windowpanes as we sat in her tiny kitchen by the stove, drinking hot chocolate and munching on her freshly baked sugar cookies. Uncle Otto seemed a bit anxious and worried. When he started talking about the folly of putting such a big lake up there on the mountains behind a man-made earth dam, Aunt Rolla shushed him up, saying it was no use frightening the girls. When the rain let up a bit, she told him to take us straight home. But this time Uncle Otto had a mind of his own. He drove around a bit to see all that was going on. A lot of people were busy moving their belongings from the first floor to the second, both in their houses and barns. They were calling to each other jovially, making jokes about the dam breaking, etc. The morning took on the air of a family picnic. Furniture, household goods and carpets were being taken up. Books and clothes and eats were being packed. Some were quickly assembling makeshift rafts, but so far, the situation wasn't really worse than it had been many a time before in Johnstown. We're used to having the rivers rising. It's just one of the trials of rainy weather in the spring.

Uncle Otto took us home then, shaking his head unhappily from time to time. He was silent and preoccupied. We were glad to be home. Most of all, glad that our house is on the hillside out of the danger of high water. Papa went downtown later, and stayed so long that Mama became worried about him. When he came back, he had lots more to tell. The rivers were now rising at eighteen inches an hour. Hundreds of families were moving out, wading through the streets with bundles of food and clothing precariously balanced on crude rafts or piled onto half submerged spring wagons. As the water rose higher, they went by rowboats. By noon the water was from two to ten feet deep, depending on which street it was measured. It was rumored to be Johnstown's worst flood on record. At eleven o'clock a log boom burst, sending a mass of big logs careening madly down Stony Creek where they crashed into the stone bridge below town. The logs jammed in among the massive arches. Soon after that the Poplar Street Bridge was washed away. Within an hour, the Cambria City Bridge went. At a church on the corner of Jackson and Locust, a funeral was being held. The water became so deep that the funeral had to be postponed halfway through the service. The casket was left in the church.

And, saddest of all, a man was drowned while trying to help a stranded family out of their house. He slipped into a flooded excavation. That was the first time a fatality had occurred in any of the floods here in our town.

Papa stopped in at the Hollis's, wondering if they needed any help. They don't expect the water to rise as high as the second floor. They don't feel it's necessary to evacuate. Dr. Dave was preparing his sermon for Sunday when the door burst open. Mrs. Bessie Oliver came in, looking badly frightened, wringing her hands and saying that the South Fork Dam is going to burst today, and the whole city of Johnstown will be washed away. Dr. Dave managed to calm her before she became hysterical. She went on her way in an easier frame of mind.

Sometime between noon and one o'clock a telegraph message came into the East Conemaugh dispatcher's tower from the next town up the valley to the east: South Fork Dam is liable to break: Notify the people of Johnstown to prepare for the worst. But no effort was made to spread the warning. In fact, two men who were shown the message laughed out loud. They didn't even bother to send the message to the central part of town.

I guess there have been too many false warnings—like in the story of the boy who cried wolf. I'll finish writing about today's happenings later; there has been so much to write about today, and I'm sure there will be more. It's mid afternoon now, and the rain is still coming down, although not as hard as before. The sky overhead seems to be lightening a little. Aunt Rolla and Uncle Otto are here—they intend to stay until all the water recedes. Uncle Otto seems very restless and uneasy. I have to wonder what's gotten into him. He keeps going to the window and scanning the skies. Then goes back to pacing the floor. Papa said that someone asked Mr. Cummins, the president of the steel company, how much higher he thought the rivers would rise should the dam break, and his carefully thought out reply was, "about two feet." That can't be too bad. I'm sure that to those who are already under water higher than they've ever been before, it could be bad enough.

It's been a long, tiresome day for the Johnstown folks. Because of the flooding the electricity is off. The gas supply is also cut off. I suppose it will be a dreary evening for most folks. I'm glad, now, for our kerosene lamps and our fireplaces. It would be gloomy and chilly without them. But already the worst is over. Papa says the water in the streets appears to be going down some. We've weathered another flood—the worst one Johnstown has ever seen. Good-by for now.

June 1

$\mathcal{E}$ ven while I was writing my last journal entry, the waters of Lake Conemaugh had already burst through the South Fork Dam and were headed toward Johnstown. Before I write about what happened when it hit, let me write about Vincent's day, helping out at the lake, as he told it to me. They did their best to avert the tragedy, but it was a losing battle.

When he arrived he was told that it had been a wild night on the mountain. Some heard, and were badly frightened by a rumbling, roaring sound, much like thunder. They were certain it was not thunder. They had never heard anything like it before! A terrific downpour followed the roaring (which some claimed was a waterspout) and the creeks got so vicious that they carried off logs that had lain there for forty years. It tore deep gullies into freshly plowed fields. Acres of winter wheat and corn that had been planted a few weeks earlier were washed away. The people up there declared that it was the mightiest downpour and the highest water ever in their memories. Every little mountain spring, run, creek and stream had turned into a rampage. There are half dozen streams and little creeks that flow into Lake Conemaugh, coming down from the Blue Knob and Allegheny Mountains. Now they seemed like raging rivers, especially the Muddy Run and the South Fork Creek. Vincent met Thomas Layton, the club employee, at the door of the clubhouse. They decided to get a rowboat up to the head of the lake to take a look at the inflowing creeks. The lake appeared to have raised about two feet overnight. The evening before, the wind had been kicking up whitecaps in the lake. Now a heavy white mist hung low over the water. By the terrible roaring they heard as they neared the head of the lake, they knew things had to be bad. The upper quarter of the lake was thickly covered with debris, logs and sawmill slabs. The water was scarcely moving. The debris was carried into an arm, or an eddy by the force of the two streams flowing in. Vincent and Thomas were astonished to see they were rowing over the top of a four-strand barbed wire fence, which stood well back from the normal lakeshore. They figured the lake must be rising about an inch every ten minutes. If this continued, in a matter of hours it could start to flow over the top of the earthen dam. It was already within two or three feet of the crest. South Fork Creek was a perfect torrent, sweeping through the woods in the most direct course, stripping branches and leaves from the trees five to six feet from the ground.

Returning to the clubhouse, Vincent and Layton were told that help was needed at the dam immediately. They went to the stable for horses and galloped off toward the dam in the cold rain. Around fifty people had gathered close to the spillway, some to help, and some bystanders gathered under the trees to watch. Along the road over the dam breast a dozen or so Italian sewer diggers were working with picks and shovels, trying to throw up a small ridge of earth to heighten the dam. Another man was trying to loosen the earth for them with a horse and a plow. But, despite the rain, the road was hard packed.

They were making little progress, and the ridge was hardly more than a foot high. At the west end another ten or twelve men were trying to cut a new spillway through the tough shale in the hillside. They were only able to dig knee deep and around two or three feet wide.

By eight-thirty things were looking serious. The decision was made that if the dam survived the day, some major changes were to be made to insure that this sort of thing never happened again. Several men went to work trying to clear away the debris, which by now was clogging the iron fish screens across the spillway, and seriously reducing its capacity. There was talk of tearing out the bridge over the spillway to pull out the big iron screens. But the decision was delayed, and by the time they had decided to do so it was too late. The screens wouldn't budge; they were so jammed in by all that debris. By eleven o'clock the water was level with the top of the dam and had already started to eat into the ridge the men had thrown up. On the outer face, near the base of the dam it looked as though several serious leaks had developed. The men exhorted to dig faster and harder; urgent orders were shouted back and forth.

At this point it was decided that perhaps something ought to be done about warning the people in the valley below. The only way was to send a man down. (The telephone line from the clubhouse to South Fork was used only during the summer season and had not yet been put in working order).

This was done. Again the warning wasn't taken seriously, and people were soon saying that there was really nothing to get excited about.

At one fifty-two p.m., another message was sent (by telegraph to Mineral Point) and from there it was wired to East Conemaugh, Johnstown, and Pittsburgh. It read: The water is running over the breast of lake dam, in center and west side, and is becoming dangerous. At two twenty-five another message was sent that read: The dam is becoming dangerous and may possibly go. Over fourteen miles away Johnstown sat, trying to make the best of a dreary situation. They had gotten all they could out of the reach of the floodwaters and there was nothing to do but wait. A leading citizen of the city was asked if he thought there really was a danger of the dam breaking. His reply was that he thinks there is, but that the water level of the rivers would probably rise only a few feet higher. How utterly wrong he was!

By three fifteen p.m., the waters of Lake Conemaugh were already plowing through the big earth dam on their way toward Johnstown. By seven past four p.m. it had traveled the fourteen to fifteen miles. I'll write about that later, and finish Vincent's story now: Shortly after noon the men began to tear up the floorboards of the bridge across the spillway to remove the fish screen. By then they were afraid to go out on the dam breast. The water had been running across the road for a while now—a good six inches deep and a hundred yards wide. It was getting stronger every minute. It was concentrated at the center, showing clearly that the dam dished a little in the middle.

When the men returned after dinner, things had taken a decided turn for the worse. Several big rocks on the outer face at the top of the dam had washed away. The water pouring across the top had cut a hole into the face about ten feet wide and four feet deep. As the water kept pouring into the hole it sliced away at the face, a little more every minute. There was absolutely nothing anyone could do now, but watch, wait and hope. They all just stood there looking at the water and the valley stretching away below. The news of trouble had spread fast and wide. A rain-drenched crowd stood on both hillsides. At about ten minutes to three o'clock there came the first break, a big notch, large enough to admit the passage of a train of cars. Next, about half the roadway fell down over the dam. Then the water just cut through like a knife. Once it got a headway it just went like a flash. After that the whole dam seemed to push out all at once. The time was three ten p.m. One of the men described it this way: (and Vincent thought it was an apt description.)

It seemed as if a mighty, destructive element had been turned loose all at once. The awful current of water leapt into the valley like a living thing. It struck the valley treetop high, snapping off or uprooting huge trees. A short distance below the dam stood a farmhouse, and in an instant it had vanished. The water advanced like a tremendous wall, sweeping giant chunks of the dam, whole trees, huge boulders and the wreckage of the farmhouse. Just beyond Lamb's Bridge, the valley turned sharply to the right and disappeared from sight. The men could only stand there, the rain beating down on them, and imagine what took place beyond the turn. They watched the level of the lake sink rapidly. It took approximately thirty-six to thirty-seven minutes for the lake to empty (someone said it was like turning Niagara Falls into the valley for thirty-six minutes). Then there was nothing left but hundreds of acres of dark ooze cut through by a violent muddy stream. The men climbed down to where the lake had been, with blankets and baskets. With cold, bare hands, they scooped up the fish that were flopping about in the muck.

I will write about what I've been told happened as the wall of lake water and debris advanced, although none of us was there to see it. The people that saw it coming and lived to tell about it, described it as a huge hill rolling over and over, judging it to be about one hundred feet high, although it was probably no more than forty feet high at that point. It was traveling at approximately ten to fifteen miles an hour, slowed down by the mass of debris that now included acres of trees, numerous mangled houses, dead animals and rubbish beyond description. If it hadn't been for all that was being driven before the water, it was estimated that it would've traveled sixty to ninety miles an hour, reaching Johnstown much sooner.

It ripped a railroad to shreds—it tore out ties and twisted steel rails into incredible shapes. At one point the valley narrowed abruptly, squeezing the great mass of water so that its front wall rose to seventy to seventy-five feet high. Some distance further it reached the viaduct, which stood seventy-five feet high and bridged the river gap with an eighty-foot arch. Debris piled against it with an awful booming crunch and sealed off the clogged arch. The water seethed back and forth, mounting up and up, until it was nearly eighty feet high. It started gushing over the top, spurting between the boulders and mangled railroad cars, ties, trees and logs lodged there. Now, for a brief instant (no one knows exactly how long it lasted) Lake Conemaugh formed again some five and a half miles downstream from its original resting place. Another dam, which, however temporary, was nonetheless as high as the first one, now held it. When this second dam let go, it did so even more suddenly and with greater force and violence than the first one. The bridge collapsed all at once, and the water exploded into the valley with its maximum power now concentrated again by its momentary delay.

A mile or so beyond the bridge was the white frame village of Mineral Point. This whole town was swept away. Onward the water rushed. The friction caused by the terrain and the rubbish caused the bottom of the mass of water to move much slower than the top. As a result the top was continually sliding over the bottom and down the front of the advancing wall. In other words, rolling over itself all the time it was pressing forward. This caused a violent downward smashing that could crush almost anything in its path. A man caught under it had no chance at all. Bodies were pounded deep into the mud.

Most of the people in Johnstown never saw the water coming. They only heard it. Those who lived to tell about it described it as a deep, steady rumble, growing louder and louder until it had become a roar like thunder, or like the rush of an oncoming train. One, who must've been farther away, described it as "just like a lot of horses grinding oats." Everyone heard shouting and screaming, glass shattering, and the earsplitting crash of buildings going down.

I can't write any more about it now. It's getting late. We are numb with shock and grief. Those who survived seem to be in a daze. Writing about it in my journal seems to be therapeutic. There is still so much more to write. In fact I hardly know where to begin and where to end in writing about the destruction of Johnstown. There was only a fringe of houses left standing at this end (ours one of them). They've all been turned into temporary boarding houses; thousands are left homeless. It's so heartbreaking to look down over the scene of destruction and death . . .

*T*he approximate time that the deluge struck Johnstown was seven past four p.m., and the devastation took only about ten minutes. But for most people, they were the most desperate minutes of their lives—snatching at children, struggling through the water and running upstairs as houses began to shake and split apart, clinging to whatever they could while the whole world around them seemed to spin faster and faster. There were also hundreds on the hillsides and on the rooftops who just stood stone still and watched in dumb horror.

The eastern end of Washington Street disappeared in an instant (and Vincent's house along with it, where we had so laboriously painted, varnished and scrubbed, only to have it all swept away in a moment). Jackson and Clinton Streets became rivers of rubbish churning headlong for the Stony Creek. Big buildings collapsed like cardboard, while smaller wood frame houses jumped from their foundations and went swirling away downstream to be smashed to bits against still other buildings, freight cars or immense trees caught by the same running current. Houses and rooftops, dozens of them with thirty or forty people clinging on top, went spinning off toward the stone bridge, which surprisingly enough, had held, despite the mountain of rubbish piling against it. The reason it held was the mountainside had taken the brunt of the water's mighty force; the bridge wasn't directly hit. Debris began piling rapidly among the massive stone arches—box cars, factory roofs, trees, telegraph poles, dead animals (from one building eighty-nine horses had been drowned and washed downstream) and hundreds of human beings, dead and alive, all washed against the wreckage caught at the bridge, until a small mountain was formed, higher than the bridge itself, and nearly watertight.

So now, for the second time within an hour, Lake Conemaugh gathered in a new setting for a while. Soon a break occurred in the railroad embankment, and some of the water began racing through it. House after house plunged through the gap. The water level in Johnstown stayed deep—thirty feet deep at some places. And the lake was spread well beyond the town. When darkness fell another nightmare began. The mountain of debris caught fire. No one knows for sure what caused it. It could have been oil from a derailed tank car soaked down through the mass and was ignited by coal fires out of dumped over kitchen stoves in the houses. Flames leapt high into the sky. It became a funeral pyre for the people trapped inside. Crashes and screams could be heard coming from the fire for a long time. There was a strange shimmering blood-red glow in the sky that could be seen for miles around. The heat from such a huge fire was intense. It burned through the night and not entirely burned out the next day. It was by far, the worst of the night's horrors, the indescribable agony of not knowing who was perishing there in the flames, and for many not knowing what had become of their loved ones.

A family, whose house was split in half at the bridge, went floating up the Stony Creek, in what was left of the attic. In the darkness that night, the Mrs. gave birth to a baby boy. The family stayed there until morning, soaked, freezing cold, the baby wrapped in a shawl.

It was a night of indescribable horrors—many were seriously injured, and those who weren't were wet, filthy and suffering from cold. There was neither food nor drinking water to be had. A number of people all had their clothes torn off. There was not much anyone could do except wait for morning, trying not to think of the agonizing scenes they had witnessed, hoping and praying for the safety of their loved ones.

With the light of dawn the next morning, small groups of people who had survived the night could be seen making their way across the muck and rubble, their eyes glazed with shock and horror at the scenes of destruction—mud, rocks and scattered wreckage, but the worst by far was the hundreds of human corpses. Papa and Uncle Otto rushed out to see what they could do to help. Mama, in her calm way, put Julie and me to cooking and preparing meals for the many homeless wanderers.

When the men came back in we received the news that Dr. and Mrs. Dave are missing. We won't give them up as lost yet. There are still places they might have been given shelter for the night. With the help of bystanders, Papa helped to rescue an old couple from the window of a half-shattered house. At first he thought it was the Hollis's, but it was someone else. Later they helped to rescue a frightened child who was floating on part of a roof.

And now, just this morning we heard that Roscoe and Meredith are missing. They had been visiting friends downtown on Main Street, and apparently were swept away with the house when it went. But we won't give them up as dead because many that were missing are still turning up alive and unhurt.

There's so much more I could write about, but I feel numb and dazed, maybe even hard and calloused toward all the tragedies we hear about. We've all been so busy taking what food and clothes we had to the needy. We're all at the point of exhaustion. Emergency morgues have been set up and opened so people can come in and try to identify their loved ones. Many people just stand around with blank and expression-less looks on their faces.

Time to go.

June 3

*M*eredith came to the door this morning, looking exhausted and bedraggled, and with a big gash on her forehead. She has an unbelievable story to tell. She and Roscoe had gone downtown to visit the

Smiths. They were sitting in the living room visiting, when they heard a terrible roar, getting louder and louder, with tremendous crashes every now and then, drowning out the yells and screams. Mr. Smith quickly threw open the outer door, and the minute he opened it, a wall of churning flotsam came crashing through. They all dashed madly for the stairway leading to the second floor, but the men didn't make it. They weren't as close. Meredith and Mrs. Smith were able to escape to the roof of the house through an upstairs window. From the rooftop they could see an immense wall of rubbish, thirty feet high. It seemed much higher, dark and squirming with debris—rooftops, huge trees, wreckage, etc. It was coming straight towards them. They watched in horror as Paxton's store was wrenched from its foundation and crushed like it was made of eggshell, and swallowed up. They saw houses lifted up and begin to roll over and over like a barrel. The roof they were on began to whirl around madly. They expected it to be washed into the deluge any minute. Buildings were scraping and grinding against each other, and being smashed to bits all around them. The thunder of destruction seemed to last for an eternity. She said the scene was like a horrible nightmare. She saw a family on a rooftop, a man, wife, and three children huddled together. They were trying to hold onto the chimney to keep from being flung into the murky depths. Then suddenly a boxcar came catapulting along. It upended for a moment, and then fell over on top of the family. A moment later she saw a man, stark naked, floating on a heap of wreckage, kneeling and praying in a loud voice, pleading for deliverance. More wreckage passed by with two girls trying desperately to keep their footing. It was tossing and rolling, and in the end they were flung into the depths. Seconds later Meredith was caught in the backwash when the wave struck the mountainside near the stone bridge. Her raft charged madly "up" the Stony Creek. The next thing she knew she was lodged between two buildings that stood intact. A woman helped her climb into a window and put her to bed there, tending her wounds. She stayed long enough to gain some strength, all the time wondering what had become of Roscoe—as we all do. There are many scenes that are too horrible for words. I won't write any more just now, except to say that we've been searching for the Hollis's. Surely they are safe somewhere. We'll find them yet.

June 4

Yesterday, just after I'd made my journal entry, Papa informed me that Roscoe's body had been found. Oh, what a severe shock! Now the children are orphans. I decided to go straight to the Eldridge house to see if I could be of any help in comforting Iris and the boys. But when I arrived, Chloe was most in need of being comforted. She had fainted dead away, as she herself put it, when they told her, and was still in bed, too dejected to get up. Iris ran into my arms and hugged me, but did not cry. The boys looked sad and hollow-eyed. Their aunt and uncle were there, and doing all right with the family.

So I started for home after staying for an hour. Papa had sent Vincent to pick me up. We drove down to the scene of most destruction, or rather, to the edge of it. People are still looking for their lost loved ones, asking after them and describing them—a five-year-old with red hair, about so high—or a wife, or a father or mother, etc. They were struggling through mountains of rubbish, trying to find a recognizable landmark in all the desolation that would tell them where their house or store had been. Sometimes there was a shout of gladness when two relatives found each other. They'd rush into each other's arms, glad to find their loved one alive. We saw an old man walking dejectedly along, trying to find safe footing with his cane. We were reminded of Dr. Dave. Oh, where could the old couple be? Vincent seemed to be as stunned and spiritless as I. We talked very little.

Oh, will this nightmare ever end? No pen can describe it . . .

June 5

It's hard to fathom it. We know for sure now that dear Mrs. Dave is gone. Dr. Dave is alive, though, and sitting in our library this minute, talking to Papa. He is in a daze. He knows his dear wife is gone; his wish would have been to go with her. He too had a tale of terror to tell. He seems to still be in a state of shock, but he says it does him good to talk about it. His story was similar to Meredith's. When the "wave of destruction" (as he called it) struck, he and his wife were taking a nap. The next thing they knew, the house was cracking apart. They were outside, their mattress floating on the rubble of churning debris. One minute Mrs. Dave was there. A railroad car floating by with a man on top caught his attention, and when he looked back his wife was gone, carried into the depths. She had been repeating a Bible verse reverently, "God is our refuge and strength, a very present help in trouble. Therefore will we not fear, though the earth be removed, and though the mountains be carried into the midst of the sea . . ." Houses were whirling by, many of them with people on the roofs. On one of them a whole group of twenty people were huddled together. It began to whirl around, and then gave a violent shudder. About half the people were knocked off. It was at this time that the break in the railroad embankment holding the newly formed Lake Conemaugh over Johnstown occurred. He saw the water racing through just as though it were a spillway. He watched house after house plunge through the break. Many were loaded with people, only to be dashed to pieces when they hit Cambria City below. (This allowed the level of the water in

Johnstown to go down, but only slowly, since the Little and Stony Creek were still pouring in tremendous quantities).

Some of the people who were sucked through the break in the railroad embankment somehow or other managed to survive the plunge. They were rescued farther down the river. Dr. Dave rode his bucking mattress through the spillway and was fished out of the river two miles downstream by men with poles and ropes. Kind people took him into their home and gave him a bed and meals until he was able to come back. He told us that two hundred people had spent the night in Alma Hall. Close to another two hundred were on the upper floors of the Union Street School, and more than one hundred on the top of the Wolfe Building. One who had spent the night thus, said that all through the night the town clock on the steeple of the Lutheran Church bonged away on the hour, just as if nothing had happened. It had a powerful effect on all who heard it. The injured lay shivering in the dark. The rooms were filled with their moaning, along with the sound of the crying of scared, hungry children, and a lot of earnest praying. Outside they could hear the noise of the aftermath of the flood; the cries for help, the unearthly howling of dogs and other animals, which added to their feelings of helpless terror. The suspense was unbearable along with all the devastation they had seen. It kept up hour after hour. They thought the morning would never come. The most horrible part of the morning was the countless dead, strewn here and there, people and animals—horses, cows, dogs, pigs, rats and even birds. I've heard that over two thousand people are estimated to be dead. But the final count isn't in yet. Many children lost both of their parents. Some poor souls have lost their spouses and all their children, too.

We attended Memorial services for Mrs. Dave and Roscoe. Many victims had no services of any kind. Hundreds of bodies could not be identified, and were buried in unmarked graves. Help has been pouring in on all sides, which is a good thing. We are still in shock; too numb for reality to really sink in. It's all just a bad dream. Soon we'll wake up and everything will be all right again, instead of this nightmare of thousands of graves being dug.

Will it ever end?

June 6

*A*nother shock: Dear old Chloe has passed on to her eternal reward. Her poor old heart just gave out. She had stayed in bed ever since she collapsed. No one realized that her end was so near. The Eldridge children's aunt and uncle need to go back to their family in Pittsburgh. At the children's request, they were brought to our home. Iris seems to be happy here. The boys, though still stunned and melancholy, seem to be adjusting well.

There is still so much to be done. The wreckage strewn across the city of Johnstown is as if everything on the nearly fifteen-mile course of the Lake Conemaugh water was dumped there. It all has to be cleaned up, searched through and burned or carted away. All the hundreds of cellars where the buildings stood were filled in by the flood, and have to be dug out; their filthy contents of reeking muck hauled out of the city. But more help is arriving every day, and with God's help, someday (though unbelievable now) it will be finished.

June 9 Sunday

Today we had sunshine. It is the first time since the flood that the sun broke through. The spring green of the hills gleamed in the bright morning sunshine. Overhead there were only a few small, soft clouds. The rest of the sky was a clear blue. The work in Johnstown went on, as though it weren't Sunday— the air rang with the sound of picks and axes, and hundreds of hammers mingled with the sound of church bells. Some whose churches were destroyed had outdoor services. Uncle Otto said that one preacher stood on a packing box to preach. He told a story about overhearing a newcomer in the valley ask a small boy how bad things were in Johnstown. The boy was said to have replied, "If I was the biggest liar on the face of the earth, I could not tell you half." The preacher told the people to give thanks that the great stone bridge had held because it saved hundreds of lives. Without it, many more would have been swept away to destruction. He also said to give thanks that the dam hadn't broken during the night. It would have been worse.

Tonight Vincent came over and was pitching a game of horseshoes with Patrick, Morgan and Papa. Julie and I watched with Iris snuggled between us. Meredith has mostly stayed in her room since we learned Roscoe is gone. I feel so sorry for her. I intend to go out of my way to be kind to her. If the dam hadn't burst, she would be up at Lake Conemaugh now with Roscoe (on their honeymoon) probably sailing on the big clear blue lake.

God moves in a mysterious way, His wonders to perform. He plants His footsteps in the sea; and rides upon the storm.

July 11

$\mathcal{T}$ oday, for the first time, I met Clara Barton. She has brought the newly organized Red Cross in from Washington to help the people of Johnstown. Papa says she's one of our best workers, or rather, the one that the people talk about the most. I've heard her called a "stiff-spined spinster."

One would never guess by looking at her that she's sixty-seven years old. She has already been through two wars. She has gone down the Ohio by river barge to help during the floods of 1884. She's been to Texas with food and supplies during the famine of 1887. She has taken her workers to Illinois after a tornado in '88, and later that same year to Florida during a yellow fever epidemic. She has set up headquarters on Prospect Hill, inside an abandoned railroad car. Miss Barton uses a packing box for a desk, from which she issues orders. She has put up hospital tents, started up temporary hotels for the homeless, and did a house-to-house survey to see just how many people need attention. I was surprised when I met Clara today. I expected her to be a big, strong woman. She's only five feet tall, and as one would expect, has a resolute mouth. She has a prominent nose and bright black eyes. Someone has described her as a keen, steadfast, powerful New England woman. I was not surprised to learn that she is a Christian.

Clara herself works almost round the clock, directing hundreds of volunteers and distributing nearly half a million dollars worth of blankets, clothing, food and cash. Papa said she seems to be everywhere at once, bouncing through the streets on a buckboard, overseeing the work. On one such ride an Episcopal priest who accompanied her thought she would be jolted to pieces, and told her so. "Oh, this is nothing," she replied, "so long as we have no bullets flying around us." She must be quite a character.

Many cases of Typhoid Fever are cropping up. Some have died of it. Quicklime is used everywhere as a disinfectant. Some day this scourge on Johnstown will be past, and the memories will dim.

Time to head for bed. We've had a long, hard day and I can't keep awake. Goodnight.

July 17

*L*abor, energy, and capital, shall, by God's grace, make the city of Johnstown more thriving than ever in the past. That's the theme of what we've been hearing these past weeks. No matter how dreadfully the valley has been ravaged, it is still "home" to the people. They plan to rebuild, and on the same spot, too. The furnaces and the steel works are all right, and the stores and shops are being rebuilt. People are working with renewed energy to rebuild their lives. Hopes run high.

Work has begun on rebuilding Uncle Otto and Aunt Rolla's house. Papa, Vincent, and the Eldridge boys are there every day. Julie and I help as much as we can. Meredith has emerged from the seclusion of her room, and started to go down every day. I think she's "setting her cap" for Vincent again because she's playing up to him, with her gay, witty repartee, and tinkling laughter—so soon after Roscoe's death. God knows we all need cheering up, so we'll let her carry on.

She'll try her charms on him again. But I'm sure that Vincent has learned his lesson well enough because he doesn't reciprocate in kind. She doesn't seem to notice, though. If she'd keep her eyes open a bit, she'd soon see that Vincent has eyes only for Julie these days. My heart rejoices for her.

Dr. Dave has gone to live with his daughter in Cresson. We miss him here, but I know he will be happier there.

Iris has become the sunshine of our home. The boys seem happy here, too.

It's a lovely evening with the fireflies flickering and a cool breeze blowing the curtains at the windows.

Julie, Iris and I are going for a walk in the orchard in the dusky twilight, so I'd better go.

August 20

*B*ig news! Julie and Vincent have announced their engagement. I am so very happy for them. Meredith must have seen it coming, but it was still hard for her to accept. She's pouting, and trying to make arrangements to move back to Philadelphia.

Another piece of good news is that Papa and Mama are in the process of adopting Patrick, Morgan, and Iris. They love it here. We've all grown very attached to them and couldn't bear to give them up. Now I can be a "real" big sister to Iris, as I had often told her. It seems too good to be true.

As for me, I don't know yet what the future holds for me—be it marriage or singleness. Whichever it is, I hope I can live in Godliness with contentment, which is great gain. I have seen first hand—at the time of the flood—how uncertain our stay here on earth is. I have seen the brevity of life. I know that when we meet the Heavenly Bridegroom face to face, it will not matter anymore whether we've been married or single. Mama and Papa say that it doesn't matter to them either. They just want whatever is God's will for their children in that matter. As long as they live noble lives of benediction to others and to themselves, that is.

I have a song, or melody in my heart again these days. Seeing a new Johnstown rising out of the rubble strengthens my faith there. I've just thought of a fitting title for my journal—"Melody of My Heart." Cheerfulness is a virtue and it's so much easier to be cheery when there's a song in your heart.

I think often of Clara Barton and her giving, unselfish life. I know I can't be a Clara Barton, but I'll do what I can for others, even if it isn't more than praying for them. More things are wrought by prayer than this world dreams of. She has been a real fountain of blessing (and others are richer for it)—a true example of living a life of happiness in doing kind deeds for others and in seeking to do God's will; truly a noble life of benediction!

In closing this journal, I'll copy a gem of a poem that Mama gave me: